VISIONS

KAT HOLLADAY

Copyright © 2016 Kat Holladay
All rights reserved.

ISBN: 1539983935
ISBN 13: 9781539983934
Library of Congress Control Number: 2016919352
CreateSpace Independent Publishing Platform
North Charleston, South Carolina

For Bob, who has always supported my ideas and my dreams.

Chapter 1
OLD TIME RELIGION

The sounds of jubilation echoed in Ruby Lynn Fortson's ears, she tried hard to keep her mind on the inspiring words coming from the traveling preacher man's mouth; but her thoughts kept wandering back to a happier time in her life. Ruby Lynn smiled, as she thought of Joe Bob Franklin. She was thirteen years old when she had first laid eyes on him; she had memorized the date, Thursday, October 10, 1957. She knew instantly a year ago, he was "The One." He was sort of tall and lanky with the most beautiful green eyes. Tommy, her younger brother, had brought him home for supper because the boys had a big football game that evening.

She vividly relived that night and how the only talk at the dinner table had been how everyone was anticipating the big game. Tommy played tight end and Joe Bob was the quarterback for the Cumberland Gap Panthers.

Her Papa had not even given the blessing before Tommy blurted out, "Shoot! I heard some of the town folks braggin' at the general store how Joe Bob was sure to get a college football scholarship if we win tonight. There are supposed to be scouts comin' to Claiborne County."

Joe Bob turned beat red and shyly answered, "Don't know about all that."

She was so excited, "Papa, don't forget you promised I can ride in the bed of the pickup truck down to Harrogate to watch the game."

He responded with a twinkle in his eyes, "Yes, sister."

Tommy shot her a puzzled look, "When'd you get so interested in sports?"

She wrinkled her nose, shrugged her shoulders, and told a fib, "Always liked football.' Tommy looked confused and scratched his head.

Holding hands was customary in her family for the blessing. Sitting next to Joe Bob had its advantages. Without thought, Joe Bob grabbed her hand and bowed his head. Before she closed her eyes, she noticed the stray curl springing loose from his Elvis Presley haircut and saw the tin of Murray's Pomade in his shirt pocket. She was not certain she liked the effect of pomade on Joe Bob's blond hair.

She was still giving Joe Bob the googlie eye when he looked up and winked at her and then promptly shut his eyes for the rest of the blessing.

She thought her heart was going to stop dead. Papa ended the blessing with "Thank you, Lord, for generously providin' us with that ten-point buck last huntin' season. In His Name, Amen." She was so keyed up; she didn't think she could eat a bite of the fried deer meat or collard greens.

The very next week, Joe Bob made her his steady and gave her his class ring. When he would sit by her on the school bus, he would brazenly hold her hand. His high school friends teased him saying he was a cradle robber. He would good-naturedly laugh at their jibes. All she wanted was to become Mrs. Joe Bob Franklin.

Ruby Lynn's day dreaming was cut short suddenly jerking her back to reality. The rusty aluminum chair where she was sitting started to tilt sideways. She and her baby nearly tumbling onto the dirt floor. Embarrassed, she quickly scanned the dilapidated revival tent to see if any of the worshipers had seen her near mishap. She sat straight up and craned her neck to the front of the tent. Her breath caught as she saw the parishioners' bodies as they swayed back and forth melodically to the twanging of the guitar strings. She witnessed how each member of the religious flock waved their hands in the air as each cried out, "Blessed be the Lord!" The chosen few stood in front of the makeshift wooden altar, throwing their heads back and speaking in tongues. The Elders' once-rigid bodies were now filled with the Holy Spirit. The preacher man hollered, "What a blessed weekend it has been for our church members!"

Next, the preacher man started singing "Shall We Gather at the River," indicating the revival was coming to an end. The group of worshipers, soaked with perspiration, began to exit the revival tent and spill into the streets. In the middle of Cumberland Gap, people stopped what they were doing and rushed to watch the celebration. If they were lucky, many were able to catch a glimpse of the worshipers as they loudly stomped their feet down the streets marching toward the river. The preacher man, with sweat dripping down his face, rolled up his sleeves and stretched out his long arms and bellowed, "Sinners One and All! Come Home to Jesus! Can I Get an AMEN?" Everyone who was following him dramatically halted and flung their hands toward the Heavens and shouted, "AMEN, Brother!"

Ruby Lynn Fortson had never really been a religious person, but now that she was a new mother she felt a need to belong to something - anything that would make her feel loved. She sheltered little Maud's eyes from the sun, tightly holding her baby close to her breast for the journey down to the river. The group enthusiastically paraded down Arthur Road, chanting Biblical scriptures. People sat fanning themselves on their front porches, waiting for the procession to pass by their homes.

Ruby Lynn hoped no one would recognize her. She had defied their small-town culture when she had kept her baby. "The One" had become "Her First" on her fourteenth birthday. Her parents insisted on a shotgun wedding but Ruby Lynn would not get married. Being a romantic girl, she bluntly told them, "My lover will come to me willingly or not at all." Rebellion, did not sit well with her family.

Her parents both urged, "For the sake of the family," that she have a stay at the nearest Florence Crittenden Mission for Unwed Mothers. Ruby Lynn retaliated, "I will not be sent away! For God's sake, I am not diseased, I am pregnant!" Her mother swooned to the floor and the conversation abruptly concluded.

Summer had ended and Ruby Lynn was excited about the upcoming school year. To her dismay, as soon as she "started showing" the local school board forced her to quit her classes.

People in the community, folks she had known all her life, shunned her. Joe Bob stopped coming around but, with her heart shattering like the stained glass of her dreams; she bravely accepted her fate; nothing was going to stop her from keeping her baby. After her memories came flooding back to her, she now had a lump in her throat, Ruby Lynn stood on the banks of the Cumberland River and realized she had gotten too caught up in the revival. She and her baby were to be cleansed of all her sins in the river. But her head started to throb and she sensed that something was wrong. She closed her eyes. *She envisioned the river currents crashing angrily against the sharp rocks on the shoreline. She had a horrific sense of foreboding that something bad was going to happen to her daughter. She could almost sense something vile lurking in the darkness of the muddy waters.* There was no way she was going to let the preacher man plunge her daughter into the foul river for a baptismal.

Quickly she made the decision to run. She took off like a jack rabbit, holding onto Little Maud in one arm and hiking up her skirt with the other. She ran as fast as she could up the steep embankment toward the other half of the crowd. She was almost to the top when she lost her footing and started to crash onto the rocks, sweet little Maud's face was smiling up at her as their bodies fell forward. In agony, she screamed, "Oh my God! Someone, help!"

Like a ghost, he appeared from the crowd, standing in front of her, his tall frame silhouetted in the sun. She was terrified that her eyes were playing tricks on her: it could not be Joe Bob Franklin. His feet were frozen to the ground; a look of horror plastered on his face. She could not believe how swiftly he reacted and sprang forward, catching her in his arms. He instinctively wrapped his entire body around their baby, to break her fall. They lay there, in each other's arms, not moving.

She reached up and wiped his blond curls from his eyes.

She looked into his green eyes and proudly declared, "What do you think of our baby girl?"

He stared down at his tiny daughter and smiled. "She's beautiful, she has your black hair." He gently touched the blond lock of hair on Maud's head. "She has a patch of mine," he noted when his daughter looked up at him and smiled.

Some curiosity seekers from town had followed the procession and had heard Ruby Lynn's call for help. She glanced up; several of the men came rushing toward her, and helped assist the couple and their baby off the rocks. She was dumbfounded at the concerned looks on their faces, and she realized she may have been judging them too harshly; not all town folk were bad people.

Next, Joe Bob did the oddest thing. He got down on bended knee and softly said, "Ruby Lynn Fortson, I know I done you wrong, but would you forgive me, and become my wife?"

The crowd silently stood watching Ruby Lynn cry tears of joy while frantically nodding her head in affirmation of the proposal. Joe Bob gently took Maud into his arms for the first time in three months. He thought to himself that he may not have been there for their daughters' birth, but from this day forward, no matter what the cost, he would lay down his life for his family. The couple was married in 1958.

Chapter 2
CUMBERLAND GAP GENERAL STORE

The newlyweds had only been married a short time when Joe Bob was jarred awake by the sound of screams from his young wife. In the blink of an eye, Joe Bob bundled up Maud and he carried Ruby Lynn down to the hospital at county seat in Tazewell. Ruby Lynn told the doctor, she had developed the headaches right after the baby was born. The doctor ran all sorts of tests, but he could not find the root of her painful headaches.

She had not told Joe the secret about her vision, she had down by the river—that is, until the day she and Joe Bob had gone shopping at the Cumberland Gap General Store. Ruby Lynn had complained of a headache a-brewing and had sent Maud over to her Mommas' house so she could lie down, but Joe Bob insisted she go with him to pick out a toy for their baby. She had selected a baby doll for Maud when she heard the door to the general store noisily bang shut. She looked up and a stranger was standing in the doorway with a boy. Ruby Lynn smiled at the boy, but he did not move; he just stood there stiff and expressionless. She noticed a large man gripping the boy's hand so tightly that the little boys' knuckles had turned white.

Ruby Lynn instinctively headed toward the boy. All of a sudden, she felt like she was going to pass out. Her arms started flailing in the air, touching the man. The touch was electrifying! *In the darkness, she saw the window open, and in that moment, she saw straight through his wicked soul.* Her eyes popped open. At the top of her lungs, Ruby Lynn began to holler, "That boy ain't his!" She started pointing to the man. "He took him from his momma and papa!" The man angrily jerked the boy's arm and started to run. Joe Bob heard all the commotion, and with the prowess of a trained athlete, tackled the man to the floor in one swoop.

Everyone present in Cumberland Gap General Store that day had witnessed how she could conjure up visions. Word spread far and wide around the Tennessee Valley how Ruby Lynn Franklin had a special "Gift."

It was only a matter of time before families started coming to Cumberland Gap. Parents desperate to find their missing children eagerly brought cherished items for Ruby Lynn to touch. Many of these families appreciated Ruby Lynn's "Gift" so very much that they offered to pay for her help. At first, Ruby Lynn was reluctant to take any reward. However, times in "The Gap" were hard, and Joe Bob had taken an extra shift down at the mine in order to feed his family, she felt obligated to take the reward money. Soon thereafter, law enforcement agencies from all over sought out her help on missing children cases. Ruby Lynn made a monumental decision to dedicate her life, to help find the missing or the dead.

Chapter 3
THE MISSING CHILD- 1959

The whistle from the mine echoed throughout the mountain, an indication that Joe Bob would soon be coming home to her.

Working in the mines had taken a toll on Joe Bob during the few short years they had been married. When Ruby Lynn looked at her husband, all her eyes could see was a tall, good-looking man with piercing green eyes, a man she loved more than life itself.

That particular afternoon, when Joe Bob arrived home from the mine, Ruby Lynn told him about the headache. He had been with her long enough to know that one of her visions would be commencing soon. He knew she had been fretting all day about the missing child, little Bess Ladd. She met him at the door with Maud on her hip, all riled up, saying, "Joe Bob, things like this don't supposed to happen here in The Gap. We're all neighbors. Police found her bike over near the Galloway place." Ruby Lynn was so upset, he made her lie down and told her he'd take care of the baby promising to wake her up before supper. But she had been sleeping so soundly he dare not wake her, so he had fed Maud and put her down in her crib.

His large bare feet slapped on the wooden floor as he paced back and forth waiting for Ruby Lynn to wake. He watched the hands of the old Seth Thomas clock slowly creep by. After he counted as it chimed eight times in the tiny cabin, he went into the bedroom to check on his wife all of a sudden, he looked down to see she was gasping for air. Joe Bob frantically cried, "Honey! Honey! Wake up!"

In the thick mist, Ruby Lynn walked slowly down to the creek. She could feel the bitter cold chill on her feet as she went deeper into the dark depths of the water below. Ruby Lynn could tell there was no coming back from this particular vision. Everything was too clear and, worst of all, she knew the child.

When Ruby Lynn saw the sweet little girl most of the mountain folks knew as Bess, she opened her arms, welcoming the small blond hair and blue eyed child to come to her. The gesture was in vain. The look in the child's eyes was vacant. It was too late for Ruby Lynn to catch a glimmer of what had happened; the window had already shut. She tried one more attempt to lure the child to her. "Come on baby girl, your'n Momma and Papa want to see you."

"Damn it!" Joe Bob frantically cried again, "Ruby Lynn, you come back to me, you hear me?" She had never been under this long and he was scared to death. He gently nudged his beautiful wife, coaxing her to wake up, but she just lay there, barely breathing and motionless in her slumber.

Magically, she must have heard her beloved's voice beckoning to her. She awakened. In his strong arms, Ruby Lynn lay sobbing. Joe Bob tried to soothe her, whispering, "Baby, I'm here, I'm here. It was just a bad dream, that tis all."

Abruptly, Ruby Lynn jerked away from him and shouted, "You know'd; tain't no dream, I done seen her! She wants me to find her and bring her home to her Momma and Poppa for a proper buryin'!" The look of hurt in Joe Bob's eyes made her gut wrench in pain. Ruby Lynn was filled with remorse. "Now, look what I gone and done to my sweet husband. I'm sorry." She watched Joe Bob lay down in their marital bed and turn off the antique lamp beside their bed. Ruby Lynn started to say something; instead she carefully covered him up with the homemade quilt her Momma had given her as a wedding present and lay down beside him.

The next morning, Ruby Lynn woke to the sound of Joe Bob chucking wood into the rustic pot-belly stove. After his Maw, had died, he had lived all by himself in the log cabin for a few years. The cabin had seen better days and he had wanted a bigger and better place to bring his wife and child. Ruby Lynn was right proud, she had a home of her own. Especially late at night, she would snuggle up real close to Joe Bob. She was amazed at how her small body would entwine with his. After all, her man stood a little over six feet tall. Oh, how she loved when he would hold her in his arms and make love to her. Those nights were special. If she were to let out a burst of joy, no one but her sweet husband would hear her cries.

She had checked on Maud who was still sleeping. Ruby Lynn tiptoed barefoot on the damp floor seeking the warmth of the pot-belly stove. She proudly scanned the room and smiled. Ruby Lynn gently touched her growing belly. Maud was going to have a new brother or sister soon. She winced as she remembered the information in her Almanac: it was going to be one of the coldest winters the people of Appalachia had ever known. Unfortunately, this news made Ruby Lynn all too aware of how many of the mountain folks would not survive the brutal temperatures.

Intently, watching his pregnant wife, Joe Bob drawled, "You gonna stand there all morning and freeze to death? I boiled you some warm milk and got a piece of chocolate to put in it, your favorite." Ruby Lynn ran and jumped square in his lap and flung her arms around his neck. "You know'd you are the best husband a girl could have?" With a big grin on his face, he took a long sip of his coffee. He cocked back his head and with that southern drawl she loved so much, he replied, "I know'd."

Ruby Lynn glanced at the clock. "Can you take Maud over to Momma's? I gots to get movin', the search party is meeting over in the field by the post office." With a worried look on his face, Joe Bob put his coffee mug down on the antique wooden table and said, "They ain't gonna find nothin' around there, are they?" Ruby Lynn did not answer; she just sighed and shook her head.

That same morning, on the other side of town, newly elected Sheriff Raymond Brooks dressed in his starched and pressed police uniform. He was alone and admiring himself in his dresser mirror. Raymond had always been large, except as he began to grow older, so did his belly. "How the hell can you carry this duty belt and run at the same time? This thing must weigh a damn ton." Ever since Raymond was a kid, he had wanted to be in law enforcement; and as luck would have it, his daddy, the Senator, had bought enough votes in this poe-dunk town to accomplish Raymond's dream. Who cared if Raymond had flunked out of the Police Academy?

He was a real sheriff, in charge of an entire town. Now, when he spoke, people would have to listen! He would show all those morons that he was somebody! Preening in the mirror, he said, "This is your first day on the job." Taking a deep breath and trying to hold in his protruding stomach, he proudly stated, "Boy! Raymond Alan Brooks, you are sure looking good!" In the mirror, his face took on a contorted expression as he shouted, "YOU ARE THE SHERIFF and YOU WEAR THE BADGE!" He glanced in the mirror as the reflection of the badge glimmered in the sunlight. Oh, how he loved to touch his sterling-silver-plated badge; it made him feel important. According his daddy, "Feeling important is what life is all about."

Ruby Lynn picked up her coat and noticed that one of the buttons was coming loose. However, there was no time to get out her mending kit; she had to meet the search party by 8:00 a.m. sharp. She pulled on two pairs of insulated socks and slipped on her worn boots. She wrapped her knitted wool scarf tightly around her neck.

She knew the drill by heart: all the volunteers must pencil in their names or make their mark on the list.

As was their routine, Joe Bob wrapped her lovingly in his arms, "Wife, you take extra care of you and that young'un you're carryin'".

Teasingly, she kissed him square on his lips, "I promise."

She hesitated a moment and continued, "Not sure how long the "Search and Recovery" will take, best eat over at Momma's".

She tugged one more time at the scarf around her neck before leaving out the door.

A fairly large crowd had gathered at the Cumberland Gap Post Office. Immediately spotting Deputy Jimmy Don Sparks' tall frame towering above the searchers, Ruby Lynn yelled, "Hey! Jimmy Don! Cold enough for ya?" He responded in his big booming voice, "I'd say, colder than a witch's tit!" Jimmy Don could always make her laugh.

"Reckon, how long will we be out here today?" she asked.

He took his deputy sheriff's hat off his head and ran his hands through his thick brown hair. He looked puzzled. "Guess that all depends on you, although I got to warn ya, the new sheriff ain't a believer."

Ruby Lynn frowned. "I had heard such. I'll let you know when I find her."

Jimmy Don looked down at his badge and smiled, "Sheriff wants to start down by the Galloway place, what'd you think?" Ruby Lynn was so focused on listening to Jimmy Don, she did not notice the large man standing near her.

Unexpectedly, he turned around. "Think about what, Deputy? I don't recall us discussing police business with civilians." Ruby Lynn visibly bristled at his rude comment.

Jimmy Don ignored the snide remark and immediately said, "Sheriff, this the woman I was tellin' ya about. This here is Ruby Lynn Franklin. Ruby Lynn, this here is Sheriff Raymond Brooks." Ruby Lynn eyed him up one side and down the other. She slowly extended her hand to the new sheriff.

Suddenly, as if he'd been bitten by a rattler, Sheriff Brooks jerked his hand back from her grasp. She watched as his eyes bulged from their sockets. Immediately he screamed, "Mrs. Franklin, I don't mean to be a naysayer, but I don't believe in voodoo or witchcraft or any of that nonsense!" His voice kept booming louder and louder. "At the Academy, we learned good detective work solves crimes!" He began laughing oddly and waving his hands wildly in the air, proclaiming, "I will allow my deputy to accompany you, since he believes in all this hocus pocus!"

After the sheriff's uncalled-for outburst, many of the searchers were shaking their heads in disapproval. Jimmy Don shrugged his scrawny shoulders, turned on the heels of his alligator cowboy boots, and followed Ruby Lynn's lead out of town. The volunteers silently began forming a search line directly behind Ruby Lynn and the deputy.

At this point, Raymond was madly scrambling around trying to gain control of "his" search party. He was livid! That Ruby Lynn Franklin had made him look like a damn idiot! It was that woman-child's fault! He'd get even with her later.

He tried to run after the group, but his heavy bulk of weight hindered the process. Huffing and puffing, Raymond abruptly halted; he was going to pass out. He touched his face and felt something wet. He realized that spittle was running down his chin and dripping on the blank signature list in his breast pocket. He could feel his cheeks turning fire-engine red.

He was desperate to gain control over the situation. He hefted his large body onto the hood of the police cruiser and frantically began waving the signature list in the air. At the top of his lungs, he screeched, "YOU HAVE TO SIGN THE LIST! IT'S THE LAW! OH! SHIT! "he screamed as he lost his footing. Awkwardly, he tumbled with a thump to the ground. Desperately, he started to dust the dirt off his badge and salvage his reputation.

Looking out of the window, the Cumberland Gap Postmaster commented, "The new sheriff is sprawled out there on our parking lot!" Laughing and looking out the post office door, one of the employees yelled, "I'll be damned, sheriff looks like a piece of roadkill lying out there!" Jimmy Don was walking across the field and smirked. "Damn, sheriff sounds like an old tom cat squalling." Ruby Lynn ignored his comment; she took her gloved hand out of her coat pocket and pointed due north toward the ridge.

The group had been searching for hours without any sign of Bess. The volunteers knew they were burning daylight, as they subconsciously picked up their pace. Ruby Lynn was almost running across the sharp rocks and the fallen timber when she muttered, "She is close now, I can feel it." Jimmy Don screamed to the group, "Careful now!" It was a signal for the group to lower their heads and watch their footing.

Ruby Lynn could finally hear the sound of the water running from the creek bed; she raised her hand in the air and the searchers stopped dead in their tracks. It was time now for only Ruby Lynn and Deputy Sparks to go alone and continue the recovery. Ruby Lynn's voice quivered, "No need for everybody to see her like that; even the dead have their dignity." Jimmy Don hesitated as Ruby Lynn tiptoed to the edge of the bank. He watched her slowly bend down and touch the water, and noticed the sad expression come over her face. At that very moment, Jimmy Don could feel time stand still; a hush fell over the woods. The missing child had finally been found.

Without hesitation, Ruby Lynn dipped her arms deep into the cold, dark water and lightly scooped up the lifeless form of the child. She took Bess into her arms rocking her back and forth. Forlornly, Ruby Lynn gazed into the little girl's face. She pushed back the strands of wet hair and said, "Poor baby, she didn't have a chance." Angrily, Ruby Lynn directly looked Jimmy Don in the eyes, and said, "This here abomination takes a special kind of EVIL."

The town was in shock at the recovery of Bess's body. Fear became an omnipresent force. After school, the dirt roads were suddenly barren of children outside playing. Folks at the mercantile store could not stop talking about the unsolved murder.

After finding little Bess, Ruby Lynn had grown despondent. Worriedly, Joe Bob saw her growing belly and shook his head and said, "Ruby Lynn, honey. I don't mean to be mean or nothin' but if we are goin' buy that crib we are goin' need that extra money." Ruby Lynn glanced at the vacant corner in their bedroom and said, "I know'd, but it don't seem right, collectin' a reward, when I ain't found out who kilt her."

Joe Bob responded, "I know'd, honey."

Ruby Lynn reluctantly replied, "I'll go over and see Jimmy Don directly."

Ruby Lynn slowly put on her winter coat and attempted to button it; however, her large belly made the chore impossible. She grabbed her hat and took off waddling toward the jail. She tried to pick up her pace as the bitter cold winds bore down from the Appalachian Mountains, thus making her journey to the jailhouse nearly impossible. Ruby Lynn was breathless from the walk; she felt her baby would be here soon.

She hurriedly opened the jailhouse door. She scanned the office and called out, "Hello!" In the corner of the office, she saw Sheriff Brooks bending down, attempting to pick something off the floor. He stooped lower and lower, his pants nearly falling down to his knees. She started to turn around and leave, but the damned cow bell on the door kept clanging and prevented her escape. Slightly embarrassed, he clumsily turned around and proceeded to pull his pants up over his huge belly; grinning like a fool, he snidely remarked, "My deputy is not here." Then he dramatically paused for a moment and said, "Oh, that's right, I guess you're here for the reward money?"

She watched as beads of spit sputtered from his meaty lips. She was unable to hide her feeling of loathing for this man. His frog-like appearance repulsed her. And most of all, she hated the way she would catch him secretly looking at her body. As if he was able to read her thoughts, he oddly croaked, "Mrs. Franklin, if I did not know any better, I'd say you don't like me very much."

She stood contemplating what to say. Ironically, the door burst open, and the cowbell started banging in her ears. Jimmy Don sauntered in carrying a cardboard box. Ruby Lynn noticed the name "Bess Ladd" scrawled in red magic marker across the side. "Howdy! Ruby Lynn!" Jimmy Don chimed. But for some reason, Ruby Lynn was unable to take her eyes off the box. Jimmy Don had set down on his desk.

The sheriff quickly grabbed his hat and jacket. "Deputy, I am headed to the bank to withdrawal Mrs. Franklin's reward money, I'll be right back."

Jimmy Don nodded as he watched the sheriff lumber out the door. "What cha' reckon spooked him so bad?"

Ruby Lynn broke her gaze from the box and said, "For some reason, he don't like me much." Jimmy Don laughed and started to pick up the evidence box. She slightly touched his arm and said, "Jimmy Don, I got to see inside that box."

Jimmy Don shifted his weight back and forth on his tall frame, and scratched his head. "Don't think that is such a good idea, it being evidence and all. Besides, the sheriff would skin me alive if he knew I let you take a look-see." She smiled up at him and he reluctantly responded, "Okay, but make it quick-like."

Jimmy Don laid the box back down upon the desk and carefully opened the lid. Ruby Lynn looked into the box and immediately pulled out a homemade doll. Stunned, Jimmy Don touched the doll in her hand and said, "That sure is weird. I don't recall no doll with little Bess when we found her. Feel it, the damn thing is bone dry." Ruby Lynn held the small doll closely to her chest and shut her eyes. *She went down deep into her soul to find the window through which she could see.*

Instantly, on this fall afternoon, she felt the warm glow on her face, and the sun was brightly shining. Gradually, she opened her eyes and there was little Bess, sitting on her bike on the dirt road and talking to the doll. "Penny, we got to hurry up and get home or we are going to be in big trouble." Ruby Lynn watched the child ride a little further down the road. Ruby Lynn felt the grit in her teeth from the dust on the dirt road. The car was coming closer and closer to Bess. She saw the man slow down and stick his head out of the car window.

"That one of those Schwinn Catalina's?" he asked.

She giggled and proudly replied, "Yes, sir. Last time, my Daddy was up at the State Capitol, he bought it for me.

The driver whistled to himself and responded, "That so? Bet he paid a fortune for that."

Little Beth shrugged her shoulders and said, "I'm not sure."

A few moments later, Ruby Lynn saw the man starting to profusely sweat.

"You know me and your daddy are good buddies."

She proudly replied, "Yes, sir. He's a lawyer."

He put the car in neutral and quickly stopped the vehicle and opened the car door. "You think he'd want you to be out here all by yourself?"

She frowned and replied, "No, sir. But I'm not alone."

He suspiciously looked around and started to close the door.

She grinned and showed him her doll. "Penny is with me."

Ruby Lynn could see the man starting to relax. He gradually hefted his body all the way out of the car and said, "Hop in and I'll take you ladies home."

Ruby Lynn shrieked out loud in terror, "Don't get in the car with him!" But it was too late, she could not stop her. Bess had already climbed in the vehicle and buckled her seat belt. The man sheepishly looked sideways at the little girl and grinned. Evil personified as he nervously jammed the car into gear making it jerk and sped off down the dirt road. "What about my bike?" were the last words, Ruby Lynn *heard.*

The sound of the cowbell clanging in her ears snapped Ruby Lynn from her vision. This was the window that she had been waiting to find; this vision had been clearer than any she had before. She now knew the identity of the killer, and she was scared to death; she could not stop shaking.

The door swung open and the sheriff entered the office, melodramatically waving the cash in his chubby hand like it was candy. "Got your reward money, Mrs. Franklin!" In a split second, his expression changed to one of a deer caught in headlights. The sheriff saw the doll dangling in her hand and loudly bellowed, "Deputy, what is the meaning of this? You know good and well that civilians are not to handle official police evidence!" The sheriff lunged for the doll and tried his best to pry it from Ruby's hand.

Ruby Lynn screamed, "She had it with her when he kilt her!"

With a stunned look, Jimmy Don loudly asked, "Who killed her?"

She replied, "I seen it all, I seen what happened! His heart is pure EVIL!"

Without skipping a beat pointing directly to the sheriff. Sheriff Raymond Brooks began to tremble and tried to back his large frame out of the door.

"She is a lunatic, she is crazy!"

Jimmy Don calmly unsnapped the strap on his holster, then steadily proceeded to pull out his service revolver. "That so? I might not have me a fancy degree in law enforcement, but it don't take no genius to figure out you took the evidence to the coroner's office."

Ruby Lynn interjected, "The doll was not there when we found her!"

Jimmy Don nodded in the direction of the gun cabinet, and said, "Ruby Lynn, you've used a 22-bolt action before, right?"

She nodded, "Yes, sir." Checking the chamber, she replied, "I see it's loaded."

At that very moment, Sheriff Raymond Brooks knew it was the end of the line for him. He realized his wicked ways had finally caught up with him and would finally do him in. Somehow, that crazy bitch must have read his filthy mind and found out Bess wasn't his first kill.

He snapped back to reality when he heard the sound of her voice say, "I've been huntin' all my life; won't think twice to kill a sorry son-of-a-bitch like him, badge or no badge." Ineptly, Raymond attempted to pull out his police .38 special from his holster and aim the weapon; he knew this was his last chance to kill them both. Raymond had always been clever; surely, he could concoct a story these ignorant mountain people would believe. After all, he was Raymond Brooks; he was The Law and he wore The Badge.

Ruby Lynn meticulously took the safety off the weapon and pulled the trigger, discharging her rifle. Raymond heard the sound of a loud pop and immediately felt a burning sensation as the bullet ripped through his flesh and penetrated into his body. He smelled the familiar scent of gun powder, the aroma of sulfur lingering in his nostrils.

Amazed, Raymond hypnotically stared down at the bullet hole. It had gone straight through his badge and into his heart. With his fingers, he felt the moist liquid oozing from his wound. He watched the dark red circle spread over his newly starched police shirt.

Mesmerized, Jimmy Don and Ruby Lynn watched as the sheriff's large body began to teeter back and forth, like one of those tin spinning tops. Raymond awkwardly swung his arm out to break his fall. As he collapsed, his hand roughly brushed against Ruby Lynn's breast. Disgusted, she gazed down at the dead body on the floor.

She looked oddly at Jimmy Don and said, "Before he died, all that bastard wanted was a new badge."

Without any emotion in his voice, Jimmy Don replied, "Go figure."

Chapter 4
FALLING APART

Ruby Lynn was in her last month of her pregnancy. Sleep had been evading her since the happenings at the jailhouse. She sat staring into the mirror on her old antique vanity, gently touching her swollen face and the dark bags under her eyes. Her rib cage felt like someone had implanted vice grips inside her, literally pulling her apart. She now realized how much her sixteen-year-old body had changed since she had become pregnant again. She finished brushing her long black hair. The luster was nearly gone and replaced with a dull tint.

She clumsily got up off her ginger cloth stool. Next, she put on her pink terrycloth robe, which lately seemed to be her only article of clothing that would cover her gigantic baby belly. The cabin seemed abnormally quiet, and she wondered aloud, "Where the heck is Joe Bob and Maud?" It was nearly time for Maud's nap. Joe Bob needed to stoke the fire in the hearth which nearly died down, causing the cabin floor to feel cold to the touch of her bare feet.

She pulled back the red and white checkered curtains from her kitchen window, solving the mystery of her missing husband and child. She observed the comical sight of her tall husband walking toward the cabin with her Momma and the town's midwife in tow. They reminded Ruby Lynn of a gaggle of geese, swarming her husband and pecking at him. Poor Joe Bob was balancing a bag of groceries in one arm and Maud in the other as her Momma followed after him, barking orders. Mabel, her midwife, was screaming scriptures from the Bible out loud to him.

As the cabin door swung open, she heard Joe Bob say, "You talk to her, she don't listen to a damn word I say! She's your daughter!"

Defenseless, her Momma retorted, "That is the very reason I brought Miss Mabel with me."

Joe Bob just answered, "Ump" to that remark.

On that note, Ruby Lynn made a beeline back to the bedroom, but it was too late. She had been caught out of bed by all three of her captors. Ruby Lynn was so tired of lying in bed and staring at the four walls. She caught a glimpse of her Momma's eyes as they darted back and forth, gauging what room her daughter had scampered into to avoid her motherly lecture. Instead, her Momma stopped in the middle of the parlor and screeched, "Ruby Lynn Franklin! Miss Mabel done tole you to stay in that bed!"

In the kitchen, caught in the middle, Joe Bob hunkered down, afraid to get involved in the discussion. The last thing he wanted was to make his mother-in-law angry. Ruby Lynn shuffled into the bedroom, and her Momma and Miss Mable zipped in behind her and slammed the door. Her Momma and Miss Mabel were like two old hens hovering over her, fluffing pillows, folding and unfolding quilts. Her Momma was making that damn clucking noise with her teeth, sucking the air in and out as she snapped at Ruby Lynn. In bed, Ruby Lynn lay there biting her tongue, not saying a word. She had a feeling what was coming next.

In one big swoop, Miss Mabel grabbed her gigantic hand bag and pulled out the Castor Oil and a wooden spoon. She methodically shoved the nasty-tasting medicine in Ruby Lynn's mouth. Ruby Lynn watched hypnotically as the excess blubbery fat under Miss Mabel's arms jiggled from side to side. From out of nowhere, her Momma interjected, "We women have to do it all, isn't that right, Mabel?"

Joe Bob made the mistake of knocking on the bedroom door. The two older women screamed, "Not now!" Her Momma was in a tizzy. She tore back the quilts and her eyes widened. "Girl! You are about to pop!" Ruby

Lynn figured this was as good as any time to bolt out of the bed and make her escape, but her Momma gave her a look and Ruby Lynn dug deeper down into the mattress. Her Momma cooed, "Now, that's my good girl. All you need is some cocoa butter to rub on those nasty stretch marks." And she gleefully squirted a half of a bottle of the ointment into her hands.

Miss Mabel opened the front of Ruby Lynn's' bathrobe, revealing her big baby belly, and exclaimed, "That young'un will be here any day now!" Ruby Lynn countered, "Good."

As Joe Bob stood there in the kitchen with Maud, all he could think about was how darn stubborn that wife of his could be. She could wear a good man down. But worst of all was the guilt he felt. He should have been the one to go retrieve the reward money; he should have never let her go alone to the jailhouse that day. Ruby Lynn was a strong woman, but lately she had been a roller coaster of emotions, laughing one minute and crying her eyes out the next. He could not just stand by and twiddle his thumbs any longer; he had to do something to prove to her that he loved her more than anything in this world.

The bedroom door burst open and out they came. His mother-in-law glared at him and scooped up Maud in her arms as she passed by him, with Miss Mabel following close behind. Joe Bob figured the coast was clear, so he stuck his head into their bedroom. He could barely see his little wife; she was covered in mounds of quilts. Ruby Lynn heard him and popped up.

She was fired up. "You would think I was ten years old, the way my Momma treats me!"

Joe Bob started to say something and she interrupted. "Momma acted like that time I got in trouble when I socked Tommy upside the head for giving my cat a Mohawk haircut." He went over to the bed, and she gave him a big smile. "You want to fool around?" She started to laugh so hard that she jumped out of bed and went to go relieve herself.

That's when it hit Joe Bob. The idea just sprang into his head as he noticed how the bedroom had somehow shrunk. Now that the two baby cribs were crammed into each corner, it was even a tighter space to try to maneuver around. He was absolutely sure how to make his beautiful wife happy, and without so much as a "Howdy You Do" he ran out the door, to the lumber yard and to swing by and pick up his brother-in-law, Tommy.

After Joe Bob, had left, Ruby Lynn searched the house for him and then she finally fell asleep, and that is when she had another one of her visions—or was it a nightmare? It was so vivid. *The road she was traveling seemed to never end. She had just neared the turn in the road and none of the landmarks seemed familiar to her. She watched as the trees bent and the bare tree limbs swirled about, and the wind started to become alive, making an inhuman howling sound. From deep in the forest, she heard an anguished cry of a child calling to her,* "Help me! Help me!"

"Oh God," she said, and she saw the beastly looking creature; it too had heard the child's cries for help. She quickly dropped onto her stomach, flattening her body against the moist ground. She shuddered at the sight of the creature's grotesque body and devilish features as it leered into the night, desperately searching for the child. She quivered as she heard its lone utterance, screaming throughout the endless span of eternity. She waved her arms as she frantically searched for the child, but the child was now gone; and Ruby Lynn was alone in the woods, lost and afraid. She could feel the evil enveloping her soul and the pounding sound in her head would not stop. She had to wake up; she had to break free from this nightmarish vision.

Amazingly, she startled herself awake. She wanted Joe Bob, she needed Joe Bob to hold her and keep her safe from the beast, but he was not inside the cabin.

She heard a noise coming from outside their cabin. Frightened, she rocked her swollen body out of the bed. She opened the cabin door, seizing the hand rail and embarked down the wooden stairs. Then she heard a familiar voice call out to her and she was no longer afraid.

"Hey Sis!" She cupped her hands to shelter her eyes from the sunlight and looked up toward the roof, and there she saw her younger brother, Tommy. Stunned, she asked, "What cha' doin' up there? Where in tarnation is my husband?"

About the same time, Joe Bob braced himself, planting his feet. He stood high up on top of the roof, near the chimney stack. "Hey honey! You sure do make barefoot and pregnant look sexy!" As she looked up at her husband, she had once again gained control of her emotions and calmed herself down. She smiled up at him and subconsciously tried to smooth her crazy hair, and looked down toward the ground and grinned. "Lord! I can't even see my feet!"

The three had a good laugh, but Joe Bob and Tommy still had not answered her question. To add to the mystery, she saw her Papa's 1955 Chevrolet pickup truck pull up in front of their cabin. Her younger twin brothers, Zach and Caleb, were perched on the bench seat in front, right next to her Papa. And to top it off, the truck bed was stacked full of lumber.

Curiosity got the best of Ruby Lynn, and she inquired, "What cha building?" Her Papa grinned and innocently answered, "Well, Mrs. Franklin, a little birdie told us you were in need of a baby nursery."

Astonished, Ruby Lynn could not believe her ears. For the first time, Joe Bob had known her; Ruby Lynn was actually speechless. She scanned the roof again for Joe Bob and she burst into tears. It all happened so quickly—one minute Ruby Lynn was smiling, and the next, she was bawling like a baby.

Tommy had never seen Joe Bob move so fast. He shimmied down off the roof like he was attending some sort of "Shivaree." All they were missing were the pots and pans to bang at the window. Joe Bob leaped to the ground, pouncing like a wild animal. He scooped Ruby Lynn up in his arms and began to kiss each tear drops on her face, then he turned and went inside the cabin and shut the door.

Embarrassed, his father-in-law looked at his three sons and asked, "What'd I say?" In unison, the twin boys responded, "Women, who knows?"

Irritated, Tommy interjected, "Twins, are you going just stand there or unload the truck?"

Hurriedly, Joe Bob took Ruby Lynn back inside the cabin. She buried her head deep into his chest and clung to him, not ever wanting to let go. Still holding her tightly, he sat down on the bed and rocked her back and forth. With tears, still in her eyes, she gazed up at him and whispered, "Joe

Bob, I'm scared. " He gently smoothed her hair out of her tear-stained face and answered, "I am too." He laid her down on their bed and he climbed in next to her, protectively covering his body with hers. He remained beside her until she had fallen asleep.

He tried to stay strong, but watching Ruby Lynn in so much pain was tearing his heart out. Maybe they should have waited to have another baby? This pregnancy had been a difficult one for Ruby Lynn; he kept having awful thoughts. What if something went wrong? What if something happened to the baby? What if something happened to Ruby Lynn? Oh, God, he thought, what if I lose them both?

Unsteadily, he stumbled outside. Wiping his tears onto his shirt sleeve. He had never in his life felt so helpless. The insurmountable burden of being a husband and a new father for the second time; bore down heavily on his shoulders.

He sat down on the wooden steps and bowed his head and he began to sob. Quietly, his father-in-law came over to him, putting his hand on his back and said, "Son, don't you worry now about our girl. She'd fight the Devil himself before she'd leave you and little Maud or let him take that young'un."

Chapter 5
BROKEN HEARTED

Ruby Lynn had felt sick all day. When Joe Bob came home from the mine, she complained, "Something ain't right with the baby, I think you need to go get Momma and Miss Mabel." He frowned and took off running out the door; he had remembered what his father-in-law had said how strong his wife was, but he too had an awful feeling something was wrong. He had quickly fetched the two women and when they arrived had taken Ruby Lynn back to the bedroom and shut the door.

Nearly an hour later, his mother-in-law came out the bedroom door, she was pale and had been crying. She looked at Joe Bob, but did not say a word, she just shook her head in despair. He stood there shaking and asked, "What about Ruby Lynn, is she going to make it?"

"God willing, she will pull through, she's lost a lot of blood, best get the vehicle ready, we're goin' to have to get her down to Tazewell as soon as possible. Joe Bob flew out the door and started the engine, then he ran back in the house and to the bedroom and gently picked up his wife, wrapping her body in a quilt spread on the end of the bed. He looked at his mother-in-law and he looked at the blood-stained sheets and said, "Throw them away." Hesitantly, he glanced over to the empty crib, Miss Mabel was still standing holding the still baby.

"It was a boy."

The doctors let Ruby Lynn go home that night, and the next day, Ruby Lynn was able to get out of bed, but her heart was heavy with the loss of her second born. Joe Bob was sitting at the kitchen table with a blank stare on his face and looking out the window. She slowly sat down across from him, the guilt was eating her up inside.

"Joe Bob, if only I had slowed down, like Momma said, our boy would be here with us right now. "

"You're not to blame, I should have never let you go alone to the jail." Forlornly, Joe Bob put his head in his hands and began to cry.

Alarmed, she carefully got up from her seat and wrapped her arms lovingly around him. She tried to remain strong, but deep down inside, the only thing she yearned for was the baby; she had lost.

She knew she had to come to terms with her loss, for Joe Bob and Maud's sake, but she realized; it was not going to easy.

It was difficult to express in words because she figured; no one would understand how she felt. Ruby Lynn's heart had been ripped out. From this day forward when she would awake, she would grieve for the lost soul of her child.

All she wanted to do was just hold her precious baby in her arms just one last time and touch her little boy. Worst of all were her feelings of helplessness.

She wondered; what kind of man he might have become?

Joe Bob stayed home for the week after they had buried their child. He took care of Maud, so Ruby Lynn could rest. Saddened, Ruby Lynn lay in bed and touched her empty belly; with tears in her eyes, she realized that life would never be the same without her little boy.

Chapter 6
THE CATS

The days seemed to fly by. Maud was doing the things most toddlers do, getting into anything and everything—and that's when something odd started to happen. Ruby Lynn had just fed Maud and had laid her down for her afternoon nap, when she heard the sound of a cat meowing. She had gone back into the kitchen to start supper. Startled, she looked in the kitchen window, and there sat three cats. She grabbed a bottle of milk from the ice box and a bowl from the cabinet. When she opened the screen door to outside, at least five cats came running into the house, whizzing by her, like they owned the place.

Ruby Lynn stood on the front porch and counted at least five more felines roaming around in her front yard. She observed that the cats were a variety of all shapes and sizes. Ruby Lynn did not realize she had left the screen door ajar; the remaining critters outside zoomed past her, headed in the direction of the baby nursery. She gave chase, and ran to get her broom to shoo them back outside. By the time she ran into little Maud's nursery, the cats were all calmly sitting down, purring and staring into the baby crib. She could not recall, but she wondered if Joe Bob liked cats.

It was late in the afternoon and Ruby Lynn was back in the kitchen finish fixing supper. She did not hear the screen door open, then she heard Joe Bob yell, "Ruby Lynn! Get in here!" Untying her apron, she ran toward the nursery. Puzzled, Joe Bob was pointing at all the cats. "Where'd they come from and what the hell are they doing in our nursery?"

She picked up the calico kitten which had entwined herself around her ankles, and playfully scratched the kitten's ears and said, "Shoot, Joe Bob, how the heck do I know? But I can tell you for sure, these critters ain't leavin' anytime soon."

At first, people in Cumberland Gap thought it was a bit odd to see a whole passel of cats prancing in a straight line, walking behind little Maud. But after a while, like most things in life, people just sort of got used to the uncanny sight; they didn't mind having to stop their vehicles to let the cat parade across the streets of Cumberland Gap. The local newspaper even did a featured spread on Ruby Lynn, Maud, and their menagerie of cats.

The hometown publicity elevated the Franklins to near-celebrity status. The men at the mine got a big kick out of the article, the men had all seen the movie "Pillow Talk" at the movie theatre, a year ago in 1959 and joked to Joe Bob that when Hollywood made a motion picture movie, they hoped Rock Hudson would play Joe Bob and Doris Day would play Ruby Lynn, and Hayley Mills would play Maud. The miners weren't sure: just how they would cast all the cats?

But what troubled Ruby Lynn most about the newspaper article was that when the reporter did the interview, she wanted to know more about her Gift. Ruby Lynn had side-stepped the question, because she did not want to let anyone know that she had not had a vision since right after she had lost the baby. She prayed she had not lost her ability, but if God deemed it so, she would just rightly have to accept it and help out in other ways.

Chapter 7
DEATH COMES CALLING

Ruby Lynn had just put Maud and her cats to bed for the night. She joined Joe Bob at the kitchen table. He was intently concentrating on cleaning his rifle, since he and Tommy and the twins were going hunting the next day. She sat down and watched him as he meticulously moved the rod with the brass brush, up and down the rifle barrel. He did not even look up from his task and asked, "What's eatin' you, Honey?"

She thumped her fingertips nervously on the old wooden table. She hesitated for a second before she answered. "You know'd, I done prayed about my Gift and all. I don't know if it means anything or not, but I got me one heck of a headache tonight."

Joe Bob finished soaking the cleaning patch in the gun oil and lightly swabbed the inside of the barrel. He carefully laid the rifle down on the table and with a concerned look, gazed into her eyes, "Best go to bed, then."

She got up and slowly turned back and said, "Whatever you shoot tomorrow, I'll make us a good stew."

Joe Bob smiled, "Sounds like a plan, I'll be to bed in a minute."

Before Ruby Lynn went to bed, she crept into the nursery to check on Maud. The cats protectively surrounded the child as she slept. Ruby Lynn was about to close the door, when she noticed the calico cat raise her head and look directly at her. The cat then sprang off of Maud's bed and followed Ruby Lynn into her bedroom.

Ruby Lynn thought the cat's behavior to be a bit strange since none of the cats ever left her daughter's side. Ruby Lynn took off her bathrobe and climbed into bed, and oddly enough, so did the calico cat, purring and snuggling close to Ruby Lynn's warm body.

Even though the writhing pain in her head would not stop, as soon as she closed her eyes, she started falling, falling down deep into the blackness. She hurled out her arms to stop from being flung into the depths of the unknown, but it was too late.

Ruby Lynn felt drowsy. She could barely keep her eyes open.

Then the vision came. It cut through her soul like a sharp knife, slicing her body open. Her mind was racing as she saw the brilliant yellow colors exploding in the darkness, and the unique blue patterns swirling around in circles. She kept seeing their faces! So many faces! She saw the girls grotesquely open their mouths, and the cry of an injured wild animal followed. She had to get out! The girls were clawing at her skin, ripping into her flesh, pulling her into the vision. She could feel their terror, as each was thrown into the abyss.

Then Ruby Lynn saw it, the EVIL in the darkness, lurking there behind the girls, taking on two human forms. Forms without faces meshed into one, and then, like magic, the forms evaporated into thin air. She peered into the thick darkness and some sort of shape appeared, and she began to trace the outline with her fingertips. It was the shape of a map.

She jerked awake. Her body was drenched in sweat, and for a brief moment, a nauseous smell filled her nostrils, the smell of decaying flesh lingered in the air. In the corner of the room, she saw the dark shapeless figure, and she saw the cat lying on the bed, cowering. The cat's fur was raised in defense and fear, and she began to hiss at the shapeless form.

Ruby Lynn crammed her back into the base of the headboard as the shapeless figure moved closer toward her, ominously motioning toward her. She tightly shut her eyes and picked up the cat and leaped from her bed.

She darted into the kitchen. Breathless and confused, she wondered why Joe Bob was still cleaning his rifle. She was unaware of how long she had actually been asleep—or did she even go to sleep? She tore open the kitchen drawer, spilling all the contents onto the floor. She got on her knees and crawled on the floor like a madwoman, screaming, "Where is it? I've got to find it!"

Alarmed at her bizarre behavior, Joe Bob jumped up from the table with his rifle in his hand. Panicked, he hollered, "What's wrong? Is Maud okay?"

He grabbed her arm, but she jerked it free. "I have to find the map before it's too late!"

Her peculiar behavior frightened Joe Bob. He demanded, "Too late for what?"

Her hands were shaking so badly that she could not grasp the folded paper map. Joe Bob reached down and quickly spread the map out on the table. By this time, Maud had gotten out of bed, hearing all the commotion. Bewildered, Maud stood in the doorway mystified as her mother poked at the piece of paper lying on the table.

Ruby Lynn choked, "There!" She pointed to the area on the map.

Joe Bob frowned and said, "Are you sure?"

In a deadpan voice, Ruby Lynn answered, "When have I ever been wrong? The EVIL is there. It is clear! Something bad happened there before and now it is startin' to happen all over again! I've got to stop it!"

Joe Bob's expression changed from one of concern to one of anguish. "But Honey, that's Arkansas."

She only replied, "I know," as she collapsed onto the floor.

Joe Bob lifted her petite body onto the sofa. Instantly, the blood began to trickle from the fresh gashes on her arms. Without thinking, Joe Bob ran to the medicine cabinet and found the gauze and wrapped it around her wounds to stop the bleeding.

It appeared to him that the visions were taking on a life of their own becoming even darker than before. Joe Bob panicked. There was no logical explanation for where she had gotten the scratches on her arms. Ruby Lynn had only been asleep for a short time, inside their house and inside their bedroom.

Just for safety's sake, Joe Bob loaded his rifle and proceeded to their bedroom. The door was slightly ajar. He boldly shouldered his rifle, ready to shoot. The rancid smell hit him, and he thought he was going to puke. He yelled, "Maud, you go outside. Don't come back in 'till I come and get you, you hear?"

From inside the kitchen, Maud loudly answered, "Yes, Sir!" And out the door she and the felines ran.

In order to breathe, Joe Bob took his bandanna handkerchief from out of his blue jean pocket and stuffed it between his nose and his mouth. He cast an eye over the bedroom, searching for the source of the smell. Then he saw the dark figure looming in the corner, and the claw like hand, signaled for him to follow.

He yelled, "Whoever or whatever, you are? You best leave now!" And without warning, in front of his eyes, the figure suddenly evaporated.

He went outside and gathered Maud and all her cats. When they reentered the cabin, Joe Bob sternly looked at Maud and said, "No one is going back into their bedrooms tonight. We will sleep out here in the living room together." Maud had never seen her Papa look so worried, so she and the cats made a pallet on the floor with the quilts that were lying on the old rocking chair from outside.

That night, Joe Bob did not go to sleep. He sat in a wooden kitchen chair, clutching his rifle and guarding his family while they slept.

The next morning, Joe Bob did not go hunting with his brothers-in-laws. Joe Bob had thought about what had happened last night, and there was no doubt in his mind that Death had come calling for his family. Fortunately, by some divine miracle, they had all survived. He could only pray that once his wife awoke, she would finally come to her senses and not leave for Arkansas. But in the pit of his stomach, Joe Bob was afraid he already knew the answer to that problem.

He was in the kitchen cooking up some vegetable soup when Ruby Lynn bounced in, chipper as a fiddle, and announced, "I'll be leavin' this evenin' and I'm takin' little Maud with me."

In the few years, they had been married, he had never cursed at her, but this time, she had pushed him too far. He yelled, "The hell you say!

Woman, have you lost your ever-lovin' mind? You are not takin' our baby girl halfway across the country!"

She glared at him and replied, "What you gonna' do? Quit your job and take care of her yourn' self?"

Joe Bob was speechless. He slammed the wooden spoon down on the counter and briskly walked out of the front door, slamming it with a loud bang! Ruby Lynn had never seen him so angry. Outside, she heard the sound of their old 1942 Desoto's engine grinding. She raced outside, yelling, "Joe Bob! Don't Go!"

He got out of the driver's seat and stood there waiting as she lunged into his arms. She did not say a word. She began to sob uncontrollably.

Neither Joe Bob nor Ruby Lynn mentioned the trip during supper, and little Maud had never seen both her parents so sad. She tried to cheer them up by telling them stories about her cats, but it was no use, so she just decided to keep quiet and eat her soup.

Joe Bob purposely waited until after supper to load up the automobile. He did not know how dependable their old 1942 Desoto would be for the trip to Arkansas. Ruby Lynn and Maud had made a special batch of sugar cookies for the trip, and had even tied a big bow around the box. Maud seemed to be the only one in the family excited about the trip. Even her cats seemed miserable.

The last piece of luggage had been loaded in the trunk and it was time to say their goodbyes. Maud petted all her cats one by one, and then gave her Daddy a big hug and a kiss. When her Mother started to climb in the front seat, Maud said, "Aren't you goin' kiss Daddy goodbye?"

With tears in her eyes, Ruby Lynn stammered, "I can't handle goodbyes."

With a heavy heart, Joe Bob blankly looked at his wife and shook his head. He slowly turned and walked into their cabin, closing the door behind him. He had done everything humanly possible to stop her from this madness; the situation was now out of his hands. There was only one thing left to do. Joe Bob dropped down on his knees and prayed to God to keep Ruby Lynn and Maud safe.

Chapter 8
1964 - THE JOURNEY

As Ruby Lynn glanced at Maud in the front seat of the car, she smiled. Maud had just turned six. Ruby Lynn was so very proud of how she was trying to be a big girl and help her Mama read the map. They were somewhere in Western Tennessee, but they had not seen a highway sign for miles, Ruby Lynn feared they were lost.

She was adrift in thought when smoke started to billow from under the hood of the automobile. Under her breath, Ruby Lynn cursed their bad luck and began to maneuver the smoking vehicle to the shoulder of the road. Ruby Lynn was grinding her teeth. She felt like her jaw was going to crack in two. She was not one to admit she was defeated, but this trip had done her in.

She frowned as she calculated in her head the amount of money left from her proceeds from her reward money. The repairs on the car would more than likely take all the money she had left. Reluctantly, she made the decision that they might as well call it quits and turn around and head back home; but what if she did not even have enough cash to get back there to Cumberland Gap.

Downtrodden, Ruby Lynn slowly got out of the car with an old rag in her hand. She carefully lifted up the scorching hood, and suddenly the smoke poured out from under the engine, temporarily blinding her. Fighting back her tears of frustration, she jumped when Maud stuck her head out of the open window and squealed, "Mama, look! The carnival's comin'!"

Ruby Lynn rubbed the tears from her eyes with her fists, and sure enough, on the horizon, a caravan of old beat-up camper trailers and an assortment of flatbed trailers carrying carnival rides were pulling up in their direction. A young fellow driving an older model truck was in the lead, and he motioned for the rest of convoy to pull over to the side of the road while he assisted the stranded woman and child.

Smiling, he jumped out of the truck. Ruby Lynn figured him to be in his twenties, but it was difficult to tell. "You ladies need a hand?"

Relieved, Ruby Lynn answered, "Mighty Christian of you to stop."

His brown eyes sparkled as he remarked, "My mother always said that one good deed deserves another. By the way, my name is Louie Youngblood, and I run this outfit."

Startled, Ruby Lynn, responded, "You are sure awful young to be a boss."

Unoffended, Louie Youngblood stated, "I got the carnival when my old man died."

Apologizing, Ruby Lynn said, "Sorry for your loss. My name is Ruby Lynn Franklin and this here is my daughter, Maud."

Ruby Lynn had not noticed her child intently watching every move Mr. Youngblood had made. Maud blurted out, "You're an Indian, right?"

He swung his long dark braids in back of his ears and grinned, "Yes, I am an Indian."

Embarrassed, Ruby Lynn countered, "Sometimes Maud does not mind her manners. Sorry, Mr. Youngblood."

Louie smiled, "Call me Louie."

He looked under the hood of the car and shook his head. "I'm goin' have to take a look underneath, if that's okay?" Ruby Lynn smiled and said, "Be my guest."

Louie took off his shirt and started to crawl underneath the engine. Maud spied the red scars all over his muscular back. Innocently, she asked, "What happened to you?" Ruby Lynn gave Maud a disapproving glare.

Louie answered, "That's another present my old man gave me," and scooted underneath the car.

Another man who was much shorter than Youngblood, but around the same age, approached, "Boss, you want me to check and see who needs gas?" Louie climbed out from under the car and answered, "Sure, Steve. Thanks."

As he was about to leave, Steve Green stared at Ruby Lynn and Maud and snarled, "Not a good place to break down. Good thing we came along."

Youngblood explained to Ruby Lynn, "The good news is, it looks like the car is repairable, I got a wrench in my truck, won't take but a minute."

Ruby Lynn was caught between a rock and a hard place. She decided she had nothing to lose, so she decided to tell Louie Youngblood about the pinch she and Maud were caught in.

"Mr. Youngblood—I mean Louie. Me and Maud are about out of money, but I need to make it to Arkansas, I have some pressin' business there."

Maud stuck her head out the window and yelled, "My Momma can see things!"

Louie Youngblood grinned at the little girl. "Is that right?" Then he turned to Ruby Lynn.

"My people believe that is a gift from the spirits."

Since Maud had spilled the beans about her "Visions," she was unsure what to say next, Ruby Lynn hesitated, "Don't reckon you have any odd jobs need tendin'? I can cook, clean and do most any work a man can."

Louie thought for a moment, then answered, "I got one tent empty. I'm in need of a crystal ball reader. You interested?"

Ruby Lynn grinned from ear-to-ear and answered, "I think I can handle that."

Maud sprang into the backseat of the vehicle and rolled down the window, and handed Louie Youngblood the box of cookies with the bow tied around it. She straightened the bow and grinned at her new friend, and said, "These are for you."   The carnival had stopped in Little Rock, Arkansas for the night and Louie Youngblood had informed Ruby Lynn, they should make it to Waldron by the afternoon. Ruby Lynn was getting anxious to finally get to their destination and set up camp.

Ruby Lynn hoped that the carnival would get to Waldron before the child was kidnapped. She had clearly seen the girl's face in her last "Vision" and she knew she would be able to recognize the child, immediately. The caravan had been traveling for several hours and, Maud finally fell asleep in the car when Ruby Lynn saw Waldron, Arkansas population 11,619 sign.

As the caravan swung down Main Street people stopped and waved and cheered at their arrival, Ruby Lynn had turned onto Danville Road, when she saw her. The little girl was walking and holding a purple leash tied on to a strange colored dog. There was no doubt in Ruby Lynn's mind this was the child, she had traveled all these miles to protect.

Her blond hair was pulled tight in a ponytail and her blue eyes sparkled with excitement as the trailers one by one passed her by. Ruby Lynn's head started to pound; she feared the child was in immediate danger; so, she broke away from the caravan and decided to follow the little girl.

Chapter 9
WALDRON

Before she started walking to town, Kitty hooked the silver studded purple collar onto her dog Blondie's neck and snapped on the matching leash she had bought her. Kitty did not have a care in the world, and she figured when the downtown shopkeepers looked out their windows they would see that, together, she and Blondie were quite a stunning pair.

She and Blondie had just passed by Dalton Insurance Agency when Kitty saw all the posters nailed on the telephone poles. The carnival was coming to town. She was about to round the corner onto Main Street when she saw the long line of cars pulling trailers. She stood there mesmerized by all the fun rides that were jammed onto the back of the trailers.

She saw a trailer hauling a "Tilt-a-Whirl" and a cotton candy machine. Today, she was supposed to go to buy a cherry phosphate drink down at the Baber Drug Store on Main Street but instead she decided to run to the Scott County Court House and tell her mother the exciting news, that the carnival was already here.

Just this morning, she had been telling her mother "Nothing very exciting ever happened in Waldron" -- unless you count the time she listened in on the telephone party line when J.B. Cobb and her daddy were talking about how J.B.'s prize Black Angus bull plowed right through the barbed wire fence on his farm and ended up flat as a pancake, dead out on Highway 71. She had already gotten in trouble a couple of times, when Miss Diane, the telephone operator, had caught her eavesdropping, but

Kitty always tried her best to muffle the handset when she put it back down on the base. And boy, did she get an earful this time. As her Daddy always said, "J.B. was just a-cussing like a sailor."

Ruby Lynn drove slowly and watched the little girl run to the back of the large building and tie up her dog to a concrete bench, then she ran up the stairs into the massive building. She parked her car in the parking lot directly behind the building, rolled down her window and waited.

For only being ten, Kitty had prided herself in memorizing the directions to her mother's office; it was the first turn to the left. She read the writing on the glass door out loud, "Scott County Social Worker," and below it her mother's name, printed in black bold letters, "Joyce Isaac."

Since her mother worked, Freda Woodard had been hired to be her keeper. Kitty loved Freda but she grew tired of Freda always reminding her how lucky she was because her mother had a college degree and was the county social worker. Freda would go on and on "Mrs. I-sack works all day helpin' young' uns find homes; she is a Do Gooder and spends all her time helping needy families."

Kitty had heard this speech a thousand times. She thought to herself, *that is all well, great and good*, but deep down inside, she wished her mother was more like her friends' mothers. They all stayed at home all day and cooked and cleaned and played bridge. If her mother was more like them, maybe she would have more time to pay attention to her.

Kitty entered the office and Bobby, her mother's secretary, was typing dictation. Bobby had beautiful brown hair and she always wore bright red finger nail polish. Kitty dreamed that one day she would be as pretty as Bobby. Bobby stopped her typing and gave Kitty a glorious smile. Kitty beamed, "Is Mommy in?" Bobby shook her head and said, "Busy."

Disappointed, Kitty turned to leave, but then she heard voices yelling inside her mother's office. Bobby knew her boss well enough that if the situation grew uglier, she would not want Kitty anywhere near her office and to get the child as far away from the office as possible.

Bobby quickly asked, "How is Blondie doing?"

Kitty grinned and answered, "You want to come see?"

Bobby took that opportunity as a good omen, and stood up from behind her desk. She had on a navy blue tight skirt and a matching cashmere sweater. She stretched her long legs. Kitty, unaware of the showdown happening in her mother's office, was more than happy for the attention and smiled when Bobby clasped her hand. Off the two went to check on the dog.

Ruby Lynn had just about given up waiting and then she saw the little girl and a woman in her late twenties come bounding down the stairs and sit down next to the dog on the bench. She figured it was about time to get back to the carnival before someone missed her and Maud, but she decided to wait just a little bit longer.

Ruby Lynn was unaware that the night before Scott County Sheriff Clyde Hankins had picked up Judah Green on an outstanding arrest warrant. It so happened Hankins knew Child Welfare—specifically, social worker Joyce Isaac—had been itching to question Green about a neglect complaint from the school, about his three daughters: Cassie, now age fourteen, Lilly, now age fifteen, and Peggy, age sixteen. Before Greens' wife had died, his office had been called out to their house dozens of times on suspected domestic abuse; but the wife would never file charges. He and Joyce only hoped Judah Green was not up to his old tricks.

Sheriff Clyde Hankins took Judah Green by the arm as he shuffled down the marble hallway to the Child Welfare office for an interview.

Hankins watched as Judah Green awkwardly used his handcuffs to brush his greasy hair from out of his eyes. He knew if anyone could get to the bottom of what was going on in the home, Joyce Isaac was his best shot to finding the answer.

Since the late 1950's, Hankins had always enjoyed working with Joyce, and here it was in 1964; and he still admired her interview tactics. Most people were fooled by her petite frame and youthful appearance, but Hankins did not have any doubt that she was one of the best in her business. She reminded him of a little bulldog—cute to look at, but don't get too close. He had seen her in action, and he knew she was capable of ripping out someone's jugular vein if they messed with the children in her foster care program and the well-being of any child in general. Plus, Joyce Isaac, being a mother herself, took her job personally.

She was gazing out the large picture window in her office and had her back to the door when Hankins shuffled Judah Green into her office. Green's eyes glowed as he saw her page boy haircut bounce in the sunlight, and then she dramatically turned and smiled. Hankins smirked as he watched her expertly weave her web of deceit. With all the southern charm of an aristocrat, she graciously welcomed the scum bag to take a seat. Demurely, she turned toward Hankins and gave him the look he had seen so many times before.

"Mr. Green, please take a seat. Sheriff there is no reason to keep Mr. Green handcuffed. My name is Joyce Isaac."

The sheriff obliged, taking Judah Greens handcuffs off his wrists. They had been in this situation more times than the sheriff would like to admit. He could instantly tell from the expression on her face that she did not like Judah Green and, most of all, that she did not trust him.

With his almost seven-foot-tall body, the sheriff stood towering over them both. Hankins was keenly aware that, the minute they had entered, the curtain had opened and the farce had already begun; Green did not have a chance but be captivated by her spell. Like the opening act of a stage production, she had deliberately been standing near the large antique glass window frame, making her appearance small and doll-like. From the beginning, like an acting script, she had studied her main character. She had already calculated that Judah Green's viewpoint on women was one of disgust. His male superiority complex was going to be his downfall.

Looking down at her leather-bound notebook, she preened, "Oh, I see you were a star athlete in high school?"

Judah Green puffed out his chest, and gave her a toothless grin, "Why ya, I was. I made the All-District team."

"And you are a decorated war hero, too! So, sorry about the passing of your wife. What was her name? Mary, I believe?"

"Yeah, I ain't got over losing my Mary. Owens, was her maiden name, her folks got lots of money. They own the drug store, here in town."

"Oh, her family was from money? So, I guess that makes you a rich man, now she is gone?"

When she first saw Judah Green, his insect-like appearance made the hair on the back of her neck stand up on end. She noted that when he was lying he would randomly scratch the top of his head, making his hair even more disheveled. She did not like the arrogant way he responded to her questions; she could bet that he thought he would never get caught doing anything wrong. In order, for her plan to work, he had to think she was an idiot; so instead of asking her secretary Bobby to bring him a cup of coffee, she personally offered to get it for him. Green had to view her as weak and subservient.

"Mr. Green, how would you like your coffee?"

He was a bit startled but uttered, "Plain black's fine with me."

She smiled broadly and nodded. "Sheriff, would you mind helping me? This door is so heavy, and I don't want to spill anything on my new outfit."

She was putty in his hands as he gave her another toothless grin as she and the sheriff left the office. Green thought to himself, "What a bimbo. It's going to a breeze coming up with a story to fool that nitwit."

He stretched out his stubby legs and was about to make himself comfortable, when he saw the picture of the little girl. He quickly stood up and hobbled over to the dusty old file cabinet, and shoved the picture frame into his pants pocket. He figured if the interview turned south, he would have a backup plan. He was not all that worried; all he had to do was stretch the truth a bit about his daughters. He chuckled to himself. He could already tell she liked him, and he was a good-looking man when he cleaned himself up.

The ignorant sheriff had tried to pin the death of his "Mrs." on him, but he had outwitted him—just like he was about to pull the wool over that woman social worker's eyes. Oddly enough, his luck never ran out, and he had already outsmarted them both. He had a picture of her kid, and unlike her dark-haired mother, the little girl had golden hair and eyes as blue as the sky.

The door opened and he could smell the fresh piping hot coffee. She innocently giggled and politely extended to him the coffee cup in her hand. He noticed her freshly manicured pink nail polish. In his deepest voice, he looked into her brown eyes and said, "Thank you, Ma'am."

Joyce leaned daintily against the massive hardwood desk, showing her shapely legs and sporting her expensive lizard high heels. She took the cup of coffee and blew the hot steam in Green's direction, making his eyes widen. Her strategy was working; unknowingly Judah Green had taken the bait. He thought, *I'll be out of here in no time; this interview is going to be like taking candy from a baby.*

"Now, Mr. Green, I see you have three daughters. Could you tell me a little bit about each one of them: hobbies, interest, that sort of thing".

Hankins was not thrilled when she had asked him to wait in the reception area outside her office, but he knew that she kept a Browning .22 automatic in her matching handbag on the top of her desk and she was not afraid to use it. After he closed the door behind him, he had already started unsnapping the strap to his service revolver for backup.

Twenty minutes had gone by when Hankins heard Green's agitated voice. "I have rights! You have no reason to hold me or get me lawyer in here!" Isaac quickly ended the interview. Hankins pulled his revolver out his holster and rushed into the office.

In the bench seat beside her Maud was starting to stir. Ruby Lynn felt a pull at her heartstrings; she missed Joe Bob so much, their poor little baby girl was exhausted from all the traveling and being away from home for the first time. She was starting to wonder, if this "Vision" had all been for not.

All of a sudden, all hell broke loose.

Ruby Lynn jumped when she saw a man with long dirty hair running fast out of the court house. Ruby observed the young woman's fear in her eyes noting the man's crazed behavior. The young woman nearly lost her balance, falling down on the ground in her tight skirt.

Shaking his fists angrily in the air and yelling at the top of his lungs, the man yelled, "You people need to mind your own damn business!"

A police officer carrying a gun bolted out the courthouse door after the man.

At the bottom of the steps, the officer yelled, "Judah Green! You go on now, or I'll have to arrest ya!"

Ruby Lynn heard the name and figured that it could not be a coincidence that Steve Green was traveling with the carnival and he had a relative here in this town.

Next the filthy-looking man passed by the young woman by the bench and the little girl saying something to them. Ruby Lynn shuttered to see the demonic look in the man's eyes. The younger woman with her body, quickly shielded the little girl from his alarming gaze.

An older woman appeared at the top of the stairs, Ruby Lynn watched as her eyes narrowed and grew dark when she saw the man near the child.

Ruby Lynn could hear the sound of the woman's high heels clicking loudly as she ran down the steep stairs. In one motion, she protectively picked the little girl up in her arms. Ruby Lynn silently watched them all as they ran back inside the court house, followed by the ever-trusting dog.

Braced in her mother's arms, Kitty sensed something bad might happen because they did not go to her mother's office. They headed straight into the office with the "Sheriff Hankins" sign on the outside of the door. Kitty realized that Sheriff Hankins had pulled his gun from his holster from the side of his belt. She watched him take a key from his gun belt, and lock the door behind them.

Inside the office, her mother set her down on the long, wooden pew bench. Kitty looked into her mother's eyes and saw her fear. For the first time in her life, Kitty realized how dangerous her mother's job was; she wished she had been nicer to her. Kitty thought, *what if something awful happened to my mother?* She looked at her mother and began to cry.

Her mother drew her into her lap, held her tightly in her arms, and said, "Kitty, you know you mean the world to me. Don't worry there is nothing I wouldn't do to keep you safe."

Kitty wiped her eyes and stopped crying. "I know, Mommy."

Once Judah Green walked to the courthouse parking lot, he sat there just watching. He snorted when he saw the big bad sheriff run back inside like a little sissy. It was time he got even with that busybody social worker and made her pay for sticking her nose into his business in the first place. Now that he had found out she had a kid, he knew exactly what he was going to do. She and that damn sheriff thought they were so damn smart, but he had outfoxed them. They had made a fatal mistake leaving him alone in her big fancy office. How stupid did they think he was? What the hell did they think he was going to tell them? He laughed out loud, thinking about how he had bold-facedly lied to them when they asked about his children and where they all lived.

He licked his dry lips as he lit a cigarette and inhaled the cool taste of Camel Menthol. Feeling clever, he thought about his next move. His sister had written to him telling him that his moron nephew—coincidently named after their worthless father, Steve—was in town working for the damn carnival. What a loser! But after all, she was his sister and kin. Reluctantly, he had agreed to talk to his nephew. Now that he had the photograph of the social workers' brat, he figured out what favor his nephew could do for him. It all depended on whether his nephew could snatch the social workers' kid. In the long run, if his nephew failed, one way or another, it wouldn't be any skin off his back.

Judah Green drew his last puff off his cigarette, pitched it out the window, and threw the pickup truck in reverse.

This had actually ended up being a good day for him. He'd have just enough time to get to the carnival and give his nephew the picture of the kid. He just hoped Steve was like the rest of the family and didn't have a conscious.

He frowned and looked down at his watch. He would barely have enough time to make his meeting. He remembered how seven years ago, he had joined the organization; back in 1957, when the government had pushed coloreds into one of the high schools up at the state capitol in Little Rock. Worried, he started driving a little faster because he did not want to be late for his Ku Klux Klan meeting.

Chapter 10
THE CARNIVAL

The next morning, the wonderful aroma of bacon cooking drifted upstairs to her bedroom. Freda must already be there. Kitty was sad her mother had already left for work. They had played cards together last night and had so much fun, but Kitty wasn't going to let what happened at the court house yesterday get her down, she had a busy day ahead of her.

She slipped her wheat-colored jeans on over her slender hips and picked up her crumpled shirt from her floor. She dashed down the stairs and ran into the kitchen. Sure, enough, Freda was standing there with her dark curly hair covered in a hair net, just like the cafeteria workers at school wore. Freda was humming and busy flipping bacon in the iron skillet on top of the stove. Being her usual obnoxious self, Kitty snatched a piece of cooked bacon off the china plate and crammed it into her mouth. "Freda, why in Jesus's name didn't you wake me up when you got here? I got to get those darned bottle caps over to Larry Earl's."

Looking through her black cat-eyed glasses, and sporting her starched apron, Freda scolded, "Don't think OUR LORD and SAVIOR has nothin' to do with your nasty bottle caps. Besides, I don't rightly re-co-llect when Mr. I-sack hired me that I was to be your'n personal secretary and con-fi-dant."

Kitty started to grab another piece of bacon, but Freda lightly slapped her hand. Today was an important day. The carnival would be opening up any time. She and her friends Linda Larson and Larry Earl

Poe had business to attend to. She went outside on the back porch and found the bottle caps sitting beside the milk box, which was full of empty glass milk bottles. A few minutes later, Freda came out on the porch and began beating one of the kitchen rugs with the back of a straw broom.

Kitty looked up at the large woman and smiled. She loved Freda Woodard with all her heart, even if the town folk called her "peculiar." By some standards, Freda was not particularly good looking. But one thing Freda could do, as she called it, was "spin a good yarn." It took Kitty a while to figure out that Freda meant she was a great storyteller. One day, she had told Kitty, "I grew up way back in the woods on Hogan Mountain in Scott County. My family had hid out there 'cause, people frown on mixed marriages. My momma married a full-blooded Cherokee, and that's where I got my brown skin and my jet-black hair and my big feet." Kitty figured that is why Freda liked to wear her Daddy's bedroom slippers, because they were large enough to fit her big feet.

Kitty was moving fast this morning and a bit agitated. She called for her dog, Blondie. Kitty had found Blondie living off the streets, half-starving and with a cut on her foot. She had made it her mission to protect her new dog from ever being abused again. Concerned, Kitty asked, "Freda, have you seen Blondie this morning?"

Freda keep beating the rug and responded, "Last, I seen her, she was eatin' that purple collar you bought her from down at the Otasco."

Perplexed, Kitty exclaimed, "What? I paid three dollars for that darn collar!" She called for Blondie and her mixed-breed dog limped up to her master. Kitty eyes filled with tears and she frowned. She looked down at the open wound on her dog's paw and said, "Why would anyone want to hurt old Blondie?"

Freda paused for a moment and bluntly answered, "Kitty, there are some bad folks out there and you best stay away from them, that is if you can help it. Best leave ole Blondie with me today, she's limpin' bad."

Kitty gently held the dog's hurt paw in her hand and responded, "We got any more of that salve Daddy puts in his hair?"

Freda threw back her head and laughed, "Not happenin'. I done been told by Mr. I-sack, you ain't to use his good hair stuff on that dog."

Distracted as usual, Kitty saw her bike leaning against the garage. "Freda, I wish I had a new bike."

Freda looked at the late-model Husky bike and countered, "Blue spray paint job looks almost pro-fession-al."

Kitty grinned and picked up the jar of bottle caps. "Larry Earl said we could trade these bottle caps in for cotton candy to the carnies."

Freda laughed and yelled at Kitty as she climbed on her bike and headed down Danville Street. "That loon Larry Earl Poe is plum crazy!"

Kitty was pedaling so fast that when she zipped into Granny Poe's yard she lost control of her bike, nearly spilling all the bottle caps. Unfortunately, she ended up smack dab in Granny Poe's prize flower bed.

Kitty was in no mood to deal with Granny Poe, so she quickly retrieved her bike and laid it up against the large maple tree in the front yard. She leaped up the two steps to the old rock house and banged on the front door. She kept knocking until she heard the sound of a voice inside the house.

"Lordy, who has come callin' this early in the morning?"

Kitty screamed, "Larry Earl, open up!"

Larry Earl was petrified that his Granny would hear her screaming, so without delay, he opened the front door. Larry Earl Poe fancied himself an actor, and without fail, every day he would dress up as a new character. Today, Kitty was not amused. They were supposed to have a meeting in the clubhouse this morning to discuss important carnival business, and here he was with his tall, lanky body with his big head squeezed into a yellow bonnet. To make matters even worse, he had bright yellow high heels on his feet.

Kitty was livid. "We don't have time for this!"

Larry Earl took out his paper fan and waved it dramatically in front of his face.

Kitty countered, "Where'd you get those shoes?"

Larry Earl just grinned and said, "What brings a Kitty Kat all the way down to Tara?"

It finally dawned on her who he was portraying today. "*Gone with the Wind*? Right?"

Larry Earl took off his bonnet and smiled from ear-to-ear. He responded, "Kitty, you are a genius! How many bottle caps we got?"

All of a sudden the front door swung open, and Granny Poe hollered, "Larry Earl Poe, what in the world you got on? Are those my good church shoes you got on those big feet of your'n?"

Like a prisoner escaping from jail, Kitty watched as Larry Earl darted around the corner of his Granny's house, with Granny Poe giving chase. It looked like a three-ring circus with them both whizzing around. Finally, Granny Poe gave out, and she breathlessly stopped by Kitty. "That boy ain't right in the head."

Kitty responded, "He's Scarlett today, from *Gone with the Wind*."

Granny Poe shook her head. Exhausted, she went back inside the house.

A few minutes later, Larry Earl came huffing and puffing from out of the backyard. "Is the coast clear?"

Annoyed, Kitty huffed, "Yes, so now can we get down to business?"

Larry Earl pulled the white shoestring that was looped around his neck, revealing a key dangling at the end. He staggered for the storage shed, asking, "How do women walk in these things?"

Puzzled, Kitty said, "Gee, Larry Earl. I'm only ten, how am I supposed to know?"

Suspiciously, he looked around the back yard and put the key into the lock. Kitty grimaced as she noticed the worn-out Superman curtains Larry Earl had used to cover the window. Larry Earl had told Kitty he was all about "ambiance." He had set up a wooden crate in the center of the room and lit a candle.

At twelve years of age, Larry Earl was not only an actor, he was a storyteller. He had told Kitty, "I am a thespian by trade and a storyteller by choice," which did not make any sense to her. She did not have a clue what he was talking about. All she knew is that her Daddy called Larry "an enigma," and her Daddy was smart because he was a teacher up at

Waldron High School. Larry would scare the bejesus out of her every time he read a story to her!

Kitty looked at her Cinderella Timex watch and asked, "I thought Linda was comin'?"

Larry Earl sheepishly grinned. "Nope, she does not like my stories." He got out his tattered spiral notebook with his name printed on the front cover and patted the bare floor. He said, "Come on Kitty, sit down." In a frightening voice, as was customary, he began.

"This story has been passed down from generation to generation, dating way back to when people used to have to stand in long soup-kitchen lines, just to get a bite to eat. The old timers here in Waldron whittling their wares on the rock wall called the 'Eagles' Roost,' just outside Crutchfield's Restaurant, swear the story is true.

"It all began one stormy night. A young couple driving down the highway found themselves in unfamiliar surroundings when they came to a dead stop at the 108 intersection near Y City and Highway 71. But for some odd reason, instead of making a right onto Highway 71 and heading due north toward Fort Smith, they turned left, going deep down south and headed in the wrong direction toward Mena.

"It was pitch black outside and the rain was pouring down. All the couple could see was nothing but dense woods on either side of the roadway. The couple had driven several miles before they realized they were lost. They were about to turn around, when all of a sudden, they thought they saw something standing in the middle of the road, further down the highway. At first glance, they thought it might have been a deer. The husband switched on his car's bright lights, and he and his wife both saw a girl.

"But it wasn't just any girl; her ghostlike appearance frightened the couple. She was surrounded by fog and her long white gown fluttered down to her toes; and her hair was so long it hung to the ground. The couple said later, 'She was there one minute and she just disappeared.'

"The couple stopped the car and searched for the girl, but it was too dark and foggy to find her; but they did make note of the mile marker.

And to this day, people say they have seen her, standing on that very same stretch of road."

After Larry Earl was finished, he touched Kitty's hair and said, "Hair just like yours."

When Larry touched her hair, she felt all jumbled up inside and her face felt hot. She quickly sprang up from the clubhouse floor and zipped out the door. Behind her Larry Earl, still dressed in his ball gown, called out, "Too scary for ya?"

Kitty did not look back. She sat up straight and tall as she pedaled her bike back down Danville Road. Her face was still warm from catching the last of the sunny breeze, or that is what she convinced herself. She slammed hard on her bicycle brakes as she squealed into her gravel driveway and flew off her bicycle.

Kitty rushed into her house. Running through her house, Kitty clamored, "Got to get ready! Tonight, we're going to the Carnival!"

Freda, mopping the wooden floors, yelled, "Whoa! Hold your horses! Floor's wet!"

Freda leaned on her mop and said, "You run this by Mr. Is-ack? Don't recall you gettin' the green light to go anywhere."

Bounding up the stairs, Kitty yelled over her shoulder, "It's okay, Larry Earl will be with me!" Kitty had never seen Freda move so fast. She threw the mop down, dumping the dirty water bucket all over the clean floor and bounded up the stairs two by two right behind Kitty.

Kitty had barely made it to her bedroom when Freda stood in the doorframe, towering above her, still wearing her Daddy's bedroom slippers. Freda pointed her finger and started shaking it in Kitty's direction, and said, "Kitty, you are not goin' to that carnival, at least not on my watch." Freda's hairnet was all frazzled and her apron awkwardly hung from her large hips.

Kitty angrily flopped onto her green and pink flowered bedspread and glared at Freda but she did not say a word; she knew the next telephone call would be to her mother up at the courthouse, and she could already guess the outcome of that conversation.

The carnival had been a whirlwind of activity all day. The tent city had magically risen and stick by stick the Ferris Wheel reached the clouds. The carnies had been assembling rides and the odor of foods cooking lingered in the air.

Louie Youngblood stood in the middle of the circle. After efficiently inspecting each tent, he looked at his watch and shouted, "Showtime in ten!" Signaling to all his employees that, ready or not, they would soon be open for business.

Maud had gone to great lengths to make a paper sign to drum up business. She had printed "The Amazing Ruby Lynn" in red ink, and she hurried outside and proudly posted the sign outside their tent, which sat smack dab in the middle of all the activity.

Ruby Lynn was putting the finishing touches on her "Gypsy" costume when Maud came back into the tent. Maud paused and her mouth gaped open. Her mother's raven hair swept down the length of her back, and a colorful silk scarf was wrapped around her head, accentuating her eyes. Her bangles and bracelets glimmered in the candle light; her mother was beautiful. Ruby Lynn smiled and slowly turned around, entwining the gold lamé skirt around her ankles and laughing. She nestled her daughter in her arms and said, "Maud, you stay close to the tent. Don't go wanderin' off. The vision is clear; it is goin' to happen here." Maud snuggled even closer into her mother's arms and answered, "Yes, Momma, but these folks seem so nice."

With a concerned look on her face, Ruby Lynn answered, "People can be deceiving."

Kitty heard Freda descend the last wooden stair. She whispered to herself, *"We'll just have to see about that. I'm going to that dang carnival."* Kitty got dressed in her favorite pair of black jeans and pulled her wrinkled Beatles musical group sweatshirt over her head and sat patiently waiting at the top of the stairs. She double-checked her watch. It was about time for Freda's late afternoon nap. She listened for the familiar sound of Freda loudly snoring. Making her getaway, and without a peep Kitty silently left the house.

Kitty decided her best plan of action to get to Linda's house would be to travel low running through her neighbors' back yard. She hunkered down her shoulders and sprinted through the Young's back yard, clearing the old run-down shed in one clean swoop. She nearly stepped on one of their wild gray cat's tails, as she expertly glided through the stack of rotten boards. Kitty was panting hard.

She was getting close to freedom because the Larson's lived in the next house, but there was only one problem: Linda's dog. Kitty usually got along pretty well with all animals, but not the Larson's red boxer. She pressed her body close to the outside of the chain link fence and scooted along the length of the fence, when out of nowhere, she saw the boxer coming. Like a snake in the grass, he slithered on his belly, planning his attack. Then he sprang high into the air, landing dead center on the metal fence pole and loudly banging his head. He only yelped once and shook his head, and fell awkwardly to the ground. Kitty leaped the fence and checked on the dog. Kitty counted her lucky stars that he was stunned and not dead.

Next, she ran as fast as her legs could take her to the safety of Linda's screened-in back porch. At about the same time, Linda opened the back-screen door and Kitty toppled inside. Confused and playing with her long brown ponytail, Linda asked, "What cha doin' in my backyard?" Kitty had a catch in her side from running and she could not talk; she motioned to the backyard and pointed. It did not take long for the boxer to recuperate. Kitty spied him, racing around the yard, growling and sniffing. Recovered from the dog ordeal, Kitty exclaimed, "Times a-tickin', we better get a move on or we're goin' miss the carnival!"

Still puzzled, Linda said, "We'd better go out the front door, we got to go get Larry Earl, anyhow."

Hand in hand, the two girls walked across the street. Kitty saw him first and her heart began to pound. Larry Earl was regally perched on a large stump. His statuesque form held his plastic saber high in the air. His purple pantaloons gently swayed in the breeze; his black pirate patch drooped over one eye. He clicked his shiny patent-leather boots together as he skillfully dismounted, landing in front of Kitty and grinning. The illusion dissolved when Larry Earl screeched in his pre-pubescent voice, "Hope we have enough treasure to get us some cotton candy."

Poor Linda had taken the bait, and she innocently asked, "What treasure?"

Larry Earl's face took on a sinister look and he hissed, "The damn bottle caps! Can't you keep up with the plot?"

Helpless, Linda looked at Kitty for an explanation. Kitty gave Larry Earl a dirty look and sweetly answered, "Linda, he's a pirate."

Larry Earl swiftly took his saber and dramatically pointed at Kitty. "Why so snippy, little Kitty? Cat got your tongue?"

Kitty snapped back, "I thought Granny Poe was comin'?"

Larry Earl countered, "Someone turning Chicken? Cluck! Cluck!" Putting his bony arms behind his back, he created a flapping noise, causing Kitty and Linda to burst into a fit of laughter.

Once again, poised Larry Earl declared, "I wore this costume to blend in with the carnies!"

The three were standing in the turn onto Mill Road, talking, when a pickup truck nearly ran over them. The driver angrily honked his horn and shouted, "Get the hell out of the road!" Before the dirt settled, Judah Green looked into his rearview mirror gripping the photograph in his hand.

Larry Earl bravely shot the finger at the driver as soon as the truck had rounded the curve. Kitty and Linda giggled. All three took off like a bullet down Mill Road as fast as their legs could carry them.

In the cool night air, Larry Earl, Linda and Kitty stood in awe. The carnival had come to life. Each inhaled the sweet smell of cotton candy and popcorn drifting from the food trailers. They were astounded when they saw the string of bare light bulbs, magically twinkling and illuminating the circle of tents. High above their heads, the Ferris Wheel buckets swung back and forth, as children squealing with sheer delight held tightly to the metal bar handles. Larry Earl grabbed Linda's hand and drug her toward the Tilt-a-Whirl.

Alone, holding the bottle caps and choking back her tears, Kitty watched them leave. They were laughing and having a great time without her. She was determined not to let Larry Earl ruin her first carnival. Freda always said "Kitty, suck it up," and that is exactly what she did. She spotted the cotton candy line and dashed to the end of the long line.

She had been standing in line there forever when one of the carnival workers poked her on the shoulder and said, "I'll take those bottle caps off your hands, if you're wanting some cotton candy?" She smiled up at the stranger, and innocently followed him toward the back of the food trailer. She thought to herself that this was her lucky day; she would show Larry Earl and Linda. She would get rid of the dang bottle caps and buy herself some cotton candy and not share any of it with them.

She was following right in back of the man when someone pulled her by her shoulders in the opposite direction and laid their hand over her mouth, muzzling her scream. Frightened, she looked up and, much to her amazement, saw a beautiful gypsy. The gypsy lady told her to follow her, saying she would keep her safe.

Kitty was confused. She wondered, "Safe, from what? And anyway, who would want to harm me? After all, I'm just a kid." Kitty felt as if she were in some sort of a dream. She and the gypsy lady were gliding in and out through the back area of the carnival tents. The gypsy lady suddenly stopped and lifted up the back of the tattered looking canvas tent. Ruby Lynn whispered, "Go on inside." Without question, Kitty obeyed.

Once inside the tent, Kitty saw a young girl sitting at a table and gazing into a crystal ball. The table was covered with a homemade quilt. Upon their approach, Kitty and the Gypsy had startled the little girl. Frightened, the little girl gazed into Kitty's eyes. Magically, Kitty was instantly hypnotized as she was drawn into the little girl's emerald eyes, watching the dancing flames from the candle light.

Kitty was shaken when, from outside the tent, she heard the ear-piercing sounds of people screaming. The carnival fell into complete darkness. Ruby Lynn reacted quickly and said, "Somebody cut off the generator. Maud, you girls get under this table and don't breathe a sound." The two girls crawled under the table and scooted close together. Ruby Lynn blew out the candle and scrunched in next to the girls, protectively putting her arms around them both, drawing them nearer to her.

Just like in Ruby Lynn's vision, the two faceless forms went roaming from tent to tent, searching, searching for the girl with the golden hair. She was the only one who would do.

The tent flap jerked opened and the two dark figures entered. Ruby Lynn saw the two shadows as they rifled through the tent. When one of the men whispered, "I thought you said the last time you saw her, Ruby Lynn had her?" The second man gruffly answered, "She ain't here."

Ruby Lynn tightened her hold on the children. As the two men left the tent, she could hear the men's rapid breathing, like ravenous animals on the hunt for their prey. Ruby Lynn tried to remain calm. She had recognized Steve Green's voice.

Ruby Lynn was the first to crawl out from under the table. She held the quilt up for the girls to crawl out. "What's going on?" Kitty wanted to know.

"Hush, they might hear you. I have got to get you out of here before they come back," silenced Ruby Lynn.

In the dark of night, the three made their way to Ruby Lynn's car, which was parked near the back of her tent. The girls were just about to open the back door to the car when the generator kicked back on and the lights once again lit up the carnival.

"There is Kitty! They have Kitty!" Larry Earl hollered.

Kitty was about to turn and run to her friends when Ruby grabbed her and pushed her into the car. Ruby Lynn quickly slammed the car door shut; jumped in the front seat and gunned the motor and sped off.

Ruby Lynn checked her rearview mirror, cringing when she saw Steve Green leaning against his truck with a look of hatred in his eyes; her heart broke when she saw Louie Youngblood standing next to him.

Larry Earl and Linda began to jump up and down and both started to run after the vehicle and began to scream, "They got my friend!" The two men leaning against the truck heard their cries for help, and the short one yelled, "You kids jump in the back, we'll try to catch em!"

Steve Green and Louie Youngblood climbed into the truck. Louie Youngblood rolled down his window and yelled, "Hold on we are going to try to catch them!"

The two children hopped into the truck bed and sped off after the car the kids were screaming and pointing to catch.

Larry Earl screamed back, "Mister! We're losing them, you got to go faster!"

The truck whipped around the curve and Linda felt herself sliding toward the open tailgate and screamed, "Larry Earl! Help! I'm goin' fall out!"

Larry Earl quickly stood up but lost his balance and with a blood curdling scream, Linda watched her friend as he careened head first out of the back of the truck, and flying out into the darkness. Linda grabbed the side panel of the truck and held on for dear life as the truck dove up an embankment, and spun out of control down into a ditch.

In the side mirror, Louie saw the boy spiraling into the air, but it was too late to stop the truck that was already spinning out of control, "Oh! Shit! We killed him!" he screamed. Linda's terrifying scream echoed eerily throughout the night sky. The truck breaks squealed as they locked up and lunged to a dead stop. Instinctively, Louie jumped out of the truck and restrained the screaming girl, covering her mouth with his hand.

From the cab of the truck Steve yelled, "Take the girl into the woods, and don't come back with her!"

"Why would I do that?" Louie asked, already panicked.

With a pistol in his hand, Steve opened the driver's side of the truck door, "If you don't have the stomach, I'll do it but remember the only reason you got to keep that shit hole carnival is because of me and my family."

Louie's luck had denigrated the minute he had met Steve Green. Louie saw the gun in Steve's hand and was all too aware of how some people were just born with bad luck. He had agreed to borrow money from Steve's family to keep his business afloat. Louie's drinking and gambling habit had taken over his life so he owed them a shit load of money. Out of fear for his own life, he had no choice but to do as Steve said. After all, the girl had seen their faces.

Grabbing Linda by the arm Louie pulled her off the bed of the truck. He could hear the sound of her jeans ripping as he quickly dragged her deep into the woods.

Louie pressed his face closely to Linda and whispered, "That man in the truck is a bad man. He wants me to kill you, if you want to live, you got to do as I say. Do you understand?"

The girl did not speak and just nodded her head.

"You've got to stay here for as long as you can. Don't scream and for God's sake, don't move!" he hissed.

Before he began to run back to the truck, Louie saw the girl wrap her arms around her scratched up legs and start rapidly rocking back and forth.

Ruby Lynn steered the car down Danville Road. This was the road in her vision, but this time she knew where it ended. Before she had completely stopped the car in the driveway, Kitty leapt out the back seat and burst into her house, shouting for Freda. Freda was pacing the floor, and came running to her cries. "Lordy! Lordy! Kitty, are you okay?"

Freda felt an odd sensation as a cold chill swept all over her body. A cool gust of wind blew open the door, and Ruby Lynn and Maud entered. Puzzled, Freda asked, "Where are Linda and Larry Earl? Weren't they with you? And who are you?"

"I'm sorry, it's all my fault, I should have never gone." Kitty cried.

"Last I saw her friends; they were jumping into the back of a pickup truck." Ruby Lynn intervened.

"Who were they with?" Freda questioned.

Ruby Lynn shook her head and said, "I am afraid they are in trouble. My name is Ruby Lynn Franklin."

In disbelief, Freda cocked her head and said, "I've heard of ya."

And without another word, Freda nodded to Ruby Lynn and went directly to the gun cabinet and tossed her one of Mr. Isaac's hunting rifles and got herself a double-barreled shotgun. She ran to the telephone and shrieked into the receiver, "This is Freda Woodard over at the Isaac house, something bad has happened down on Mill Road send an ambulance now!"

Freda put her two fingers to her mouth and loudly whistled for the dog. As if sensing the danger, Blondie came limping into the room.

Freda bent down and told the little girl with the green eyes, "This here is Kitty's dog. She may not be much to look at, but she loves her Kitty, and she will protect yawl or die tryin'." Eyeing the door, and putting her full weight on her injured paw, the dog circled the girls and froze still, ready to attack. Her low growl rose up deep inside her chest.

Freda cautioned, "Lock the door behind us. I already called the sheriff. He is on his way to pick up Mr. I-sack from the baseball park. They should be here any minute. Tell them I had to go, and I'll explain later." The girls grasped each other's hands and nodded.

Chapter 11
THE SEARCH

The women left the house and headed back toward Mill Road. They were feeling the tension in their necks as they rode in silence, searching the dirt road for the children. Suddenly, Freda frantically pointed to the ditch on the side of the road and hollered, "Tire tracks over yonder!" Ruby Lynn slammed on the brakes, grinding the gear into neutral, as Freda took her rifle from its sling, anticipating the danger she might face. Freda jumped out and immediately saw Larry Earl's lifeless body lying at an odd angle, with his head pressed against a large rock. "I'll tend to the boy! You go find the girl!"

The sound of thunder echoed in Ruby Lynn's ears and she felt a chill go up her spine as she started walking into the dense forest. Unlike in her vision, this time the demons had faces and she knew their names. For the girl's sake, she only hoped she was not too late.

Linda sat alone shivering in the dark. The cold rain started to pour down upon her, and then hail started pelting and bruising her body. Earlier, she thought, she had heard the sound of the truck with the two men leaving. She was not sure how long she had been out there in the woods. But at this point, she was not taking any chances, and she dared not move.

The sound of a siren screamed throughout the night. Linda wondered if maybe someone was coming for her. Her heart sank when she realized that no one even knew where she was hiding. She was scared to death. She had tried to be brave, but she could no longer fight back her tears. She desperately wanted her Mommy and Daddy to come get her. Uncontrollably, she started shaking from head to toe. She heard something coming through the thick brush. So as not to scream, she bit down deep into her lip, tasting the warm blood in her mouth. The lightning flashed, and Linda saw the dark figure with the rifle slowly approaching, and she was terrified. Death had come for her.

Freda heard the ambulance siren coming. She stepped out into the middle of the road and waited to flag the emergency vehicle down. Freda discerned that, with a head wound so severe, she could not move Larry Earl. She had to wait for trained help to show up. Worst case scenario, even if the ambulance did come, she was unsure of the whereabouts of Ruby Lynn and Linda, and she did not want to leave them out there all alone.

Bravely, Freda stood in the middle of the gravel road and started to wave her hands in the air. "Stop! For God's sakes, stop!" She prayed the ambulance would see her first and not run her over.

The Emergency Medical Technician checked Larry Earl's vitals and moved him carefully onto the gurney. He explained to Freda that he would have to drive Larry Earl up to St. Edward's Catholic Hospital in Fort Smith in order to get him the care he needed.

Freda heard a rustling sound coming from the dense brush and saw Ruby Lynn carrying Linda Larson in her arms.

Ruby Lynn screamed, "I found her like this! She's got no visible signs of being hurt, could be internal!"

The EMT paled at the sight of the limp body and hurriedly called into the ambulance radio, "I've got a 10-78, do you copy?" He winced when the voice on the other end of the radio replied, "Copy that. Nearest ambulance in route will be coming from Greenwood. That will take at least twenty minutes."

Hearing the news, the young EMT was so rattled that Ruby Lynn was afraid he was going to faint before he was able to drive the boy to the hospital. She did what she did best: started to take charge of the dire situation.

Ruby Lynn barked, "Young man, you get in there and you drive like the Devil is after you. I'll follow you with the girl in this vehicle. You got that? Freda, afraid you're goin' have to wait here for more help to arrive." They both nodded and the E.M.T. obediently got in the driver's seat of the ambulance and slammed the door. Without hesitating, he ripped the ambulance into gear and took off, and not looking back.

The sound of the lone siren echoed throughout the night as the two vehicles raced down Highway 71 to their appointed destinations. Ruby Lynn pressed down hard on the accelerator, trying to keep up with the speeding ambulance. She held her breath as she navigated the slick curves on the two-lane highway. She kept checking her rear-view mirror in the hope Linda's condition would change, but the little girl's body just lay there in the back seat, listlessly.

At the Scott County and Sebastian County lines, at speeds approaching over one hundred miles per hour, Ruby Lynn zoomed past an Arkansas State Trooper who was parked in the empty Dairy Queen parking lot. Ruby Lynn was unaware Sheriff Hankins had already radioed ahead, a "10-33" coming in from Scott County. The state trooper in the cruiser instantly turned on his running lights, siren, and fell in behind her. The blue lights ominously swirled in the darkness.

An emergency situation had taken over the road, and other cars quickly pulled over to the side of the highway. It seemed like they had been driving down a street called Townsend Avenue for hours, instead of minutes, when Ruby Lynn saw the ambulance turn on to a street named Rogers Avenue and she saw the tall hospital building looming to her left, with the large cross on top of the roof. She was speeding so fast that she slid into the side entrance of the Emergency Room, nearly knocking over two carts and lifesaving equipment monitors.

Upon their arrival, Ruby Lynn was overwhelmed as she watched the trauma crew of trained nurses and doctors spring into action. She was positive that angels had been riding with her in the car tonight, and that only by the Grace of God had she somehow managed to deliver the girl safely to the hospital.

As she got out of the vehicle, her legs started to wobble. She held on tightly to the hand railing leading to the hospital. She stayed with Linda until the nurses whisked her away.

Ruby Lynn saw a crucifix mounted above a door, and a sign marked "Chapel." Unsteadily, she entered, dipping her fingers into the Holy Water and crossing herself. She clasped her hands together to pray, and walked slowly down the aisle and sat down.

Ruby Lynn closed her eyes as the "Vision" consumed her. She felt a cold breeze whip through her soul and her vision misted as other forces took over. She saw Maud slowly coming toward her. Maud smiled at her, and Ruby Lynn held out her arms to embrace her daughter; but her soul passed straight through her, entering into another side, a place unknown to Ruby Lynn. The "Vision" hit her like a Mack Truck slamming into a compact automobile. Her heart almost stopped and the only words she said was, "Maud". Oh, God!

Chapter 12
JUDAH'S LUCKY DAY

Since all the hoopla from the Civil Rights Movement on the television and radio, The Grand Giant was just discussing why the Klan needed to ensure Waldron remained a sundown community, the sound of the sirens wailing interrupted the KKK meeting. Since several of the members were pillars of the community; they had to take their leave.

Judah Green laughed to himself, secretly knowing what had just transpired at the carnival but not sharing that particular information with his brethren. He was headed out to his truck when one of the other members called out to him.

"Green, you got a minute?"

Judah looked back and it was one of his old buddies from high school football days.

"What's up, Ed?"

"Got an opportunity for you, interested? Let's take a ride in your truck."

Judah had always heard the rumors that had surrounded Ed Holloway, but he had just chalked it up to the town gossips who had too much time on their hands. As the two men drove, Judah listened intently to the bizarre story Ed Holloway had told him about the Black Fork Mountains. Judah knew no one in their right mind could make this shit up. This opportunity might be the answer to Judah's problems with the law.

Ed had just told him about his "Home up among the wilds of the forest."

A place where no one dared to enter, and if they did, they would never come out. He explained it was sort of like the Klan only better. The mountain men had rules and a council to govern their community. But what he told Judah next was just crazy.

"All our women folk got blond hair and blue eyes, and this way we can make damn sure, our race will stay pure, and since you got three daughters with the "Golden Hair" you all will fit right in."

Judah Green, could see no problem with that reasoning and smiled. This was his lucky day.

Chapter 13
THE KIDNAPPING

Steve Green and Louie Youngblood were counting their lucky stars. They had been able to push the truck out of the ditch, and the old piece of junk's engine had actually started. They had made it to the stop sign by the Waldron Bank and turned left onto Main Street. They had just passed the Plemmon's department store when Louie Youngblood, sitting in the passenger seat of the old truck, had an epiphany of sorts.

He was contemplating: at what point in his life had he become a total screw-up? Then he scowled at Steve Green, reminding him of the answer to that question. Somewhere down in Mississippi, he and Steve had gone into town and found a high stakes poker game.

He had been up until the last hand, he held two Aces high and he was sure, he had counted all the cards in his head but the booze had clouded his judgment. Unfortunately, he had gotten too cocky and had wagered the carnival as collateral. A damn card game had changed the course of his life.

The cop car, with sirens blaring, whizzed by Steve's beat-up old pickup truck. Louie had done some downright bad things in his life, but he felt this situation was hopeless.

Now he found himself running from the law. He should have known the cockamamie story Steve Green had told him was an out-and-out lie, especially when he showed him the picture of the little girl with the blonde hair and said she was a relative of his and someone had stolen her, and was mistreating her.

Louie had a soft spot for little kids. He knew all too well what it was like to be born into a lousy family. He loved his Maw but she was no match for his crazy father and eventually, she had given up and left, leaving him there alone with his old man. As an adult, he had made an unspoken vow that if he survived his old man's beatings, he would never hurt a defenseless child. So, when Steve asked him to help save the little girl, he had no problem helping get her back to her family. He would be a hero in the family's eyes and yet now, that fantasy had turned into a morbid reality of kidnapping, death, and betrayal.

Back in Waldron, he had purposely let Steve think he had murdered the little brown haired girl. To make matters even worse, he had not even helped that boy who fell out of their truck. In all likelihood, the poor kid probably had broken his neck. Yeah, he was in too deep now to get out, so after all he had sacrificed to keep his family carnival business afloat, he had to leave it behind and go hide out. The last instructions Steve's uncle gave him was to meet them at a diner in Y City.

Steve's instructions were to bring the girl. For some reason, she was special. Louie apprehensively wondered what kind of greeting they would receive from Steve's uncle? Especially when they showed up empty-handed without the girl? Louie concluded that his Uncle Judah Green, being from the same gene pool, was probably even crazier. Louie had witnessed first-hand already how nuts the one sitting next to him driving the damn truck acted.

To top it off, Steve would not shut the hell up. "Those Waldron fuzz are as dumb as rocks," he laughed. "Here we are sittin' right under their noses, like sittin' ducks, and they have no idea we are the ones they are lookin' for." He paused for only a moment and continued to babble like they were on an episode of *Dragnet* or something, "Ain't even put up no road blocks or such."

Fortunately, they only had seen the one police car. They easily made their way down Highway 71 toward Y City and pulled into the parking lot of the diner there. Louie looked in and saw a waitress with a huge beehive hairdo handing out menus to some customers in a booth. Louie's stomach growled. He tried to remember when he ate last? They sat there and waited a few minutes, until a beat up old truck pulled up beside them. He could see a man and three girls crammed on the bench seat. A short stocky man with a cigarette hanging from his mouth got out and came toward their truck. Steve jumped out and shook the man's hand. Louie saw the expression on Judah Green's face darken and knew they were in deep shit; no girl, no safe place to hide. Steve's shoulders were hunched over as he got back in the truck.

"He says, if we don't come back with the damn girl, we are both dead. Chief, if you open your mouth and try to run, I will kill you myself."

Youngblood was trying to keep his cool but after that statement lost all his composure. In his mind, he was visually grabbing Steve by the throat and strangling him to death. *I*nstead he asked, "Now what are we supposed to do? We can't go back to the carnival. Ruby Lynn, knows it was us who tried to take the girl!"

"Uncle Judah said we go back and we take her. Nobody will expect a second attempt so soon. There is a flashlight in the glove box."

As they sat in the parking lot, Louie started to read the handwritten directions out loud. The Black Fork Mountain Wilderness overlaps the Oklahoma-Arkansas border just west of Mena. Climb up the east side of US 270. The weather is bad that far up the mountain." What burned most in Louie's mind was the last sentence: *"If you get lost, no one is going to come looking for you, and besides the bears will more than likely kill you."* Steve turned the truck around and headed back toward Waldron. This time, his uncle, had given him the address to the girl's house.

They took the county roads back to town and parked on the street behind the Isaac's house. The backyard was huge. The tall trees and bushes cast a shadow on the two men crouching in the dark, waiting.

There was only one car and a squad car parked in the driveway. After an hour, the squad car left, no sirens no lights. Steve could see a man through the window, looked like he was dressed in a baseball uniform and an old lady. With them were two girls, not just the one, which might be a problem.

Pretty soon, the two adults and the two children came outside, got into the vehicle in the driveway and drove off. After the last botched attempt, Louie was going to have to do the thinking for both of them because he was now convinced that Steve did not have a brain in his head.

"Okay, if they are gone, they have got to come back. Cops are gone so we move the truck and park it closer to the house. We hide behind the garage and we take down her old man and then get the kid."

It was not long before the car returned. The children climbed out of the car first. Before they could even slam the door, Louie was on them. He caught the girl in the picture first. She started to scream but he slapped his hand over her mouth. When he realized the second child was Maud, he started to hesitate.

"This is Ruby Lynn's girl."

"I don't give a shit; she's seen us so we gotta take them both."

Louie caught Maud and she started to kick and bite. He had both girls in his arms and lost his balance slamming the three of them, pressing their faces down hard into the gravel lined driveway.

The man in the baseball uniform jumped out of the car and started running toward Louie and the girls. Steve sprang into action and tackled him to the ground, punching him in the face and beating him until he was nearly unconscious. Louie screamed, "Damn it! Don't kill him".

Louie picked up Maud and the other girl from the gravel, wincing when he saw both were bleeding. He did not say anything and headed for the truck with Steve following hot on his tail.

Steve stepped on the gas. Louie took the tape from out of the glove box and wrapped it tightly around both girls' mouths and shoved them down to the floorboard where no one could see them.

Louie Youngblood knew, with that single gesture, he sealed his fate forever. The two girls were whimpering with tears flowing from their eyes. Louie leaned down toward the floorboard and whispered, "I won't hurt you, everything is going to be all right". When Steve realized, what Louie was doing, he yanked one of Louie's braids and hissed, "Don't talk to them."

Louie and Steve did as they were instructed. When they came to the intersection a few miles outside of Mena, they drove the truck deep into the forest and left it there. Before they started their ascent up the mountain Louie demanded, "We're in the middle of nowhere; I'm taking the tape off their mouths." Steve just shrugged, "Whatever."

On foot, and with the two girls; they started their climb up Black Fork Mountain. The terrain was steep. They had been climbing for hours and had not seen a soul when it struck Louie Youngblood that they were hopelessly lost.

Chapter 14
JENNY

The cabin lay at the very top of the Black Fork Mountains. Most of the mountain folks had always called the woman who now lived there "Jenny"; now that she was living alone, without her Mister. She was not sure that "Jenny" was her real name, but she had been living up on the mountain as long as she could remember and, for some reason, that is what her Mister had always chose to call her.

Looking out the window of her cabin, she could see the three crude headstones, covered in weeds, out among the pines. One was her Mister's. She often wondered if the other two graves were where her Ma and Pa had been laid to rest? Unfortunately, she could not remember their faces either. She did not think she had been born up on the mountain, but she reckoned that when it was her time and the Good Lord called her home, that she would spend all of eternity here.

Years ago, her "Mister" had told her, he had found her lying in Big Creek, near dead. He was a healer, and it was his duty to bring her up the mountain to his cabin. He had saved her life. Her Mister had always been kind to her; he was not like the other mountain men, with their "Golden Hairs." When she first came to live with him, he had taught her the healing ways. Now her long, once-blond hair was streaked with wisps of gray. Many of the mountain folks told that she was the oldest of the Golden Hairs. With this nobility, she was held in high regard among the Misters, and every male on the mountain was forbidden to touch her.

After her Mister, had passed, many of the men folk remarked that, for a woman, she had proved to be an excellent healer. And since her Mister had passed, the mountain men would see fit to send their Golden Hairs up to her place at night, to set on her porch big baskets of fresh food and berries for her to eat. Once a week, she would pack her healing pouch and camping provisions, and hike down the mountain to check on all the Golden Hairs. She was not quite sure where all the Golden-Haired girls came from, or how they arrived. Over the years, the only thing she had observed was that every once in a while, one would just appear at one of the mountain men's cabins. Jenny felt sorry for the girls. While their Misters were not looking, she would try to sneak them food. She was always called if one of the girls became sick. She would be allowed to heal their beaten bodies. Another one of her tasks, the one she enjoyed most, was to serve as a midwife when it was child-bearing time.

She heard old Pete coming up the path, yelping. She loved that darn beast, even if he did try her patience. If he had tangled with a skunk today, he was in for a rude awakening because he was not going to set foot in her cabin without a good scrubbing. She and the wolf had a history; she had rescued him when he was just a mite of a pup. He was the runt of the litter, and his pack had abandoned him in the woods. She and Pete had been together ever since; some of the folks were a bit skittish around him, but he was gentle as a lamb with Jenny.

She had gone outside to fetch the wooded bath barrel when, in the distance, she heard the rapid succession of muffled gunfire. The alarm had been sounded: strangers were among them on the mountain, and it was time to get armed and ready.

She shooed the wolf inside, barring the wooden door with the two-by-four she kept in the corner by the fireplace. Jenny took her Winchester 30/30 down from above the cook stove and sat quietly in her rocker, with Pete standing stiffly beside her. She watched as the hair started to bristle at the back of his neck. His hackles vibrated as he guarded the only door to her small cabin. She softly patted his neck, and heard the low growl coming from deep down in his chest, reaching his throat. The wolf could smell the unfamiliar human scent the wind was pushing up the mountain. She had no doubt that Pete would rip apart any stranger that dared to enter her home or attempted to harm her.

The blasts from the weapons echoed over the mountain, making Steve Green jump in terror. "Where the hell is that comin' from?"

Louie stood still listening and attempting to gauge the distance. Louie yelled to Steve, "Shut up!"

Panicking, Steve cried, "We got to find my uncle! He'll tell them who we are!"

Louie scanned the area and saw the overgrown path leading up the mountain. He was not naïve; he knew the odds of them getting off this mountain alive were slim to none. Madly, he started to run for his life up the path and dragging Maud behind him. The woods were thick. Steve and Kitty were following closely in back of him. Louie picked up Maud and sprinted up the path, the jagged thorns protruding from the harsh underbrush angrily slashed open his bare skin.

His hopes of being rescued from the remote woods were about to be utterly dashed, when in the distance, he heard the sound of a lone train whistle. Hysterically, he rushed toward the shrill sound in the vast unending forest. As the prickling briars gouged through his shoes and into his feet, he could feel his warm blood trickling from the harsh gashes in his skin.

The cool wind started to cut through the trees. It seemed that the higher up Louie climbed, the stronger the gusts of wind grew. Eventually, the echo of the train subsided in his ears. Disoriented, he was afraid the mountain had been playing tricks on his mind. Directly in front of him, he saw smoke billowing whimsically into the sky. Once again, he feared, this was his imagination.

He briefly paused and put his hands on his knees to catch his breath from carrying Maud. A few feet behind him, Steve was running so fast he nearly collided into his backside. Crazed and overwrought, Steve whined, "Why the hell are you stopping?" Louie did not answer and pointed into the sky in the direction of the smoke stack. Steve brusquely rammed him out of his way, dragging Kitty in back of him and Louie fell awkwardly to the ground, nearly landing on Maud. Stunned for a moment, Louie sat there noticing the frost covered leaves, an obvious sign that temperatures were drastically falling. From the exposure to the bare elements, he was starting to lose feeling in his hands and feet. Before that idiot Steve got them, all killed, Louie jumped up and tried in vain to catch up with him.

At first, Louie could not see the sturdy little cabin nestled among the pine trees. The only indication the structure was occupied was the smoke rising from the rock chimney.

As the group approached, Pete's ears perked up inside the cabin. The wolf had heard the strangers' footsteps crushing the pine needles. He lunged toward the door, knocking over the two-by-four in his path. Urgently, Jenny tried to block his way with her small body. She whispered, "No! Pete. Down." Growling, the animal backed slowly away from the door. Jenny edged closer to the crack in the open kitchen window and carefully braced her rifle barrel on the window sill. She shouted, "Don't come any closer or I'll kill you where you stand!"

Louie had caught up with Steve and the girl. Once Louie heard the woman's command he immediately halted and threw his hands up in the air, and Maud stood shaking from the cold air. Awkwardly, Maud grabbed Kitty's hand, yanking it from Steve Green as he ran forward. The girls stood trembling in the cool wind, only hoping for some kind of miracle. Unaffected by the command, Steve kept barreling up toward the entrance of the cabin. A shot rang out, hitting the toe of his boot. He grabbed his foot and screamed, "Son of a Bitch!"

The door creaked open, and out stepped an almost child-like woman. As the harsh wind blasted through the air, her skirt swirled delicately around her petite ankles; her long blond hair majestically flowed to the ground. In contrast to her small size, a giant wolf stood beside her.

The scuff on Steve's boot toe proved that the woman knew how to shoot. After the first shot was fired, she confidently moved closer to them. Louie gawked as she positioned her feet firmly on the earth. She expertly hugged the wooden stock of the weapon, molding it tightly into her shoulder. She carefully raised the gun barrel, adjusted her rifle sight aiming it straight at Steve's forehead.

Louie could not believe how fast it all happened. One moment Steve was running, and in the next moment he had pulled a knife out from his boot and was screaming and charging toward the woman. With his teeth bared, the wolf lunged toward Steve. Hitting his mark, the animal bore his teeth down deeply and viciously into Steve's arm. Steve cried in pain, but he was unable to shake the wolf off his arm. Steve slammed the blade into the wolf, and even as the wolf's blood gushed from the stab wound Pete's jaws mercilessly tore flesh from the bone. Again, Steve slammed the knife blade into the wolf breaking its hold, kicking the beast into the tall grass.

Louie saw the bloody knife blade gleaming in Steve's hand and bolted toward him. Simultaneously, the vibration from a rifle shot rang in Louie's ears. He dove onto Steve's back. Clutching the knife in his bare hands, Louie jerked the sharp blade from Steve's grasp and pitched it into the brush. The second blast from the weapon riddled Steve's body. He stumbled, falling backwards, and landing heavily upon Louie. Steve's dead body trapping Louie.

Louie saw the blood pouring from the wound in his hand. Jenny cautiously walked over toward him and brushed back his braids from his face, Louie saw her bending over him. The last thing he saw before he lost consciousness was her piercing blue eyes.

Something in Jenny told her to save the Indian. She knew that by nightfall the temperature would drop. If she left him outside, he would freeze to death. Something kept nagging at her; she had never seen a brown man before. He had tried to stop the other man from hurting her. She motioned toward the girls to come help aid her in rolling the dead body off of the Indian. The younger girl came over to help her, but the older one appeared to be in shock and just kept staring at the dead body.

It was a struggle for the two of them to move the injured man back into her cabin. He weighed twice as much as either of them did and was so very tall. Once inside, she checked the deep gash in the palm of his hand. She had to stop the blood loss or he might well die. She looked at the two little girls; Jenny recognized they were both uncontrollably shivering, so she quickly bundled them up in animal fur blankets and sat them in front of the roaring fire.

She hurriedly fetched her healing bag and took out the bandages and the herbs. She skillfully began to dress the damaged area. She felt the stranger's forehead. He was already burning up with fever. Immediately, she tore off his clothes and drug him onto a fur-skin pallet on the floor. She gently touched his beautiful brown skin, which glistened with perspiration. She flushed at the sight of his taut muscles covering his magnificent body.

Earlier, Jenny had checked on old Pete, who was no worse for the wear. He only had a slight nick in both of his ears. Jenny was taken aback when Pete uncharacteristically laid down on the pallet next to the injured man. It reaffirmed, in her mind, her solid judgment that this stranger would not harm her. She really was not sure what her next move would be if the stranger recovered. All she knew for now was that she would tend to his needs.

It was getting dark outside, and she had about waited too late to move the dead body to the shed. The last thing she needed was for the bears to smell the scent of death. Hungry for food, the animals would be too dangerous for her if they came lumbering up the mountain near her cabin.

Jenny wondered about the identity of the dead man. She asked Pete, "Why on earth do you think those two men were trespassing up here and what are they doing with those two little girls?" She was bound by Mountain Law to report the shooting, and tomorrow she would have to go down the mountain and seek out the Elder Council. It would be up to the Council to determine if Jenny had a rightful kill. Then there was the problem of what to do with the Indian and the two girls.

The next morning, the sun shining through the kitchen window woke Louie Youngblood. He had been having the wildest dreams. He was still groggy as he rolled over and felt the warm breath on the back of his neck. He lazily opened his eyes and gazed into a pair of blue eyes. Instead of those steel blues belonging to the woman, they belonged to a wolf, who was curiously looking at him. He recalled from the past that the best solution, when dealing with a wild animal, was not to move. His confusion mounted as he glanced underneath the wolf's body and saw his bandaged hand.

He heard a creaking sound beside him. He looked up and saw Jenny sitting propped up in an old wooden rocking chair. "How ya feelin'?" she drawled, rocking back and forth.

At first he was unable to answer her question, his throat was so dry, but he cleared his throat and gruffly answered, "Where am I?"

She gave him a smirk and countered, "Black Fork Mountain, don't you remember?"

He still had not moved a muscle and his arm was still pinned under the giant beast. His thoughts were muddled as he tried to recall the last few hours. He once again looked into her piercing blue eyes and was jolted back to reality. He was speechless as he admired her sharply chiseled facial features. She was even more beautiful than he recalled.

She looked at him oddly and said, "My name is Jenny, and I reckon you got some explanation why you and that dead man were trespassin' on my end of the mountain and what you doin' with the young' uns?"

His hand was throbbing in pain. In anguish, he asked, "Could you call off the wolf?"

Annoyed, Jenny explained, "His name is Pete." Then, without a word, she nodded toward the animal and he gingerly stood up. Still a little wary of Louie, the animal did not take his eyes off of him.

"How are the girls?"

"Suspect they've seen better days, but I got them to eat a bite and then they finally fell asleep. Neither one said nary a word."

"My name is Louie Youngblood. Steve Green is the one you killed. We were coming to see his uncle Judah Green."

She scowled at the mention of the Green name. She scoffed, "Well, dang it! He and his girls is fairly new to the mountain; but I heard tell, he is one crazy son of bitch. That's going to be more trouble than I had bargained for. Good thing you lived. You'll have to testify it was a warranted kill."

Puzzled, Louie wondered, *"Who on this godforsaken mountain is in charge?"* He started to stand up, but he was butt naked from head to toe. He muttered, "Where are my clothes?"

Boldly, Jenny commented, "Had to strip you naked, you were burning up with fever. Ain't nothin' I haven't seen before. I'm what they up here call a healer. I fix most livin' things."

She tossed him some men's clothes.

Louie examined the unfamiliar clothes. Jenny stated, "My Mister was about your size. You are welcome to borrow his."

Disappointed, Louie asked, "So you are married?"

Jenny's blue eyes twinkled, "Never been married."

Eagerly, she gave a full and detailed account to Louie of how she had come to live most of her life up on the mountain. After she finished, Louie half wondered if his fate would be the same. Would he never leave? Then it occurred to him: after all that had happened in Waldron, what better place to hide from the law? Besides, he could personally make sure nothing bad happened to Kitty or Maud.

Jenny put on her heavy coat made of fur pelts and ordered, "Best get dressed. You, me and Pete got to haul your friend down the mountain to his kin."

"What about the girls?"

"Nobody usually comes up here, unless it's an emergency. They'll be safe for now."

While he was dressing, Louie looked out the small kitchen window and spotted Jenny connecting a travois onto the back of the wolf. For some curious reason, he felt proud that the woman used the Native American custom to haul things, even if it was being used to transport the dead body of Steve Green. As if she could sense him standing at the window, she yelled, "Grab that fur jacket off the bed. You're goin' to need it for the trip!"

Louie opened the small cabin door and a gust of wind nearly knocked him down. It was unmistakable; the seasons were dramatically changing. The bone-chilling wind engulfed his body. The view from this level was breathtaking. High overhead in the blue sky an eagle soared. Amazed at how the gusts of wind bent the tall pine trees nearly to the ground, he contemplated how the trees could withstand the years of frigid winds whipping through their branches and still remain standing.

During the descent down the path following Jenny, Louie watched her expertly guide the drag sled down the rigid decline. The fresh air and warm sunshine felt good on his face as he maneuvered down the path, but the uneven rocks jarred his body. By the time they had reached their destination, he was trying his damnedest not to let Jenny see him wincing and writhing in pain.

The three had just entered the clearing when Louie saw the run-down shack. He thought he saw a girl poke her head above the cracked window. The shack's door opened, and a man holding a sawed-off shotgun stepped out and started briskly walking toward them. The wolf snarled, baring his teeth at the man, who shouted, "State your business, Healer!"

Jenny immediately started undoing the leather leashes around the wolf's body and quickly grabbed her rifle from the travois. She planted her feet firmly on the ground, bringing the rifle butt up to her shoulder, and yelled, "Afraid I got bad news. I got your nephew here but he be dead."

Louie saw the undeniable look of hatred fill Judah Green's eyes. He pointed the sawed-off shot gun in their direction and swiftly closed the gap between them.

Jenny stood her ground. Quickly, Louie stepped in front of her, shielding her from the approaching man. Louie did not falter. He looked Judah Green straight in the eyes. "Leave the woman be, it was a true kill." Noiselessly, Jenny's wolf touched the side of his leg; he could hear a menacing growl coming from the beast.

Suddenly, Green stopped and his eyes grew large. Louie had not heard them; they were like apparitions when they had appeared. The three were wearing dark clothes and holding weapons. They had silently come out of the woods and were standing shoulder to shoulder beside Louie.

The larger man boomed, "Green, you heard the Indian. The Healer made a true kill. Let her be." The man motioned with his weapon for Jenny to move back.

Green snidely asked Louie, "Did you get the "Golden Hair"?"

Jenny was beside him now. Louie felt her flinch. He glared at Green and answered, "There are two, one dark haired, one golden."

Green smiled, "I'm only interested in the gold."

Looking at the Elders, he stated his case, "My nephew died bringing the Golden Hair to me and I want her."

The tallest man in the group commented, "So be it. The Healer will bring the girl to you in the morning."

Jenny started to protest but she knew not to question a decision made by one of the leaders.

Green spouted, "Indian, don't belong here."

Jenny rebutted, "He saved my life; I'll be accountable for him."

Louie stood his ground and never moved. He would accept whatever decision, these men concluded.

The taller of the three Elders demanded to speak with him.

"Indian, what do they call you?"

"Louie Youngblood."

"The Healer has spared your life but do not think we will not kill you if you try to go back down the mountain."

Louie Youngblood nodded, "I understand." He turned around toward Jenny. As silently as they had come onto the property, the Elders were gone.

For the time being, Louie was still alive, and he had been dismissed. Jenny, Pete and Louie were turning to leave when the door to the shanty opened slightly. A girl with dirty hair, clad in filthy clothes, meekly came out. Green screamed, "Get back inside!" The girl quickly obeyed. Shocked, Louie stared at Jenny, but she did not blink an eye and kept a steady pace back into the woods.

It was a silent journey up the mountain. Jenny had much on her mind. It bothered her that Louie had not been forthright and had not told her the girls had been abducted. She had never condoned the clan's customs, but she wondered why he would do something like that?

Truth be known, she was mighty lonely living all by herself now. She could not keep her eyes off of Louie. She had never felt this way about a man before in her life. She was aware that every time she looked at him, her heart would stir.

It had unnerved her when he had stepped in to protect her from Judah Green. Her Mister had always taken care of her, but this was different. She knew deep down inside Louie Youngblood had sacrificed his life twice to save hers. She wondered: is that love? Or did he just pity her and feel obligated to her for saving his life?

She had overheard what the Elder had said to Louie, and she hoped he would abide by their rules. She knew all too well what happened to those who disobeyed their authority, and it was not a pretty sight. Unfortunately, she knew the truth about the girls, sooner or later, she was going to have to defy "The Council" and help get the two off the mountain.

During the trip, up to her cabin, Louie could not take his eyes off Jenny. He was afraid she was angry with him, and all he wanted to do was make things right. He had never in his life felt this way about a woman. It was strange; he knew the moment he first saw her that he could not live without her by his side. He could almost close his eyes and see her standing there, on the mountain with the wind blowing in her hair. All he wanted to do was to hold her and touch her. Ironically, he felt a need to protect her, even though she had apparently been doing a good job of that on her own.

They had hiked up to the clearing when Pete let out a howl and raced toward the cabin, eager to be home to see the two little girls. Jenny was relieved seeing the cabin door still closed. She had hoped Maud and Kitty were too afraid to leave the cabin. She figured they had no idea where they had been taken and desperately wanted to go home. Jenny was aware at their young ages, the girls probably grasped the likelihood of being returned back home, impossible. The customs on the mountain were strict. In order to stay alive, Jenny would have to stress to them each must do as they were told.

The next day, Jenny had to tear Kitty from Maud's arms, she was screaming and crying, but Jenny knew unless she made good on her promise; Judah would go straight to the Elders and then all three of the strangers' lives would be in jeopardy.

Life upon the mountain for the girls, would prove challenging but Jenny was good to Maud. She never raised her voice. Jenny treated her like she was her own but deep down inside Jenny knew the truth. The girls belonged back with their parents. She hoped since Judah had three girls of his own, he would not hurt Kitty. That night after Maud went to sleep, she spoke her concerns to Louie.

"Louie, you know I've never been off the mountains since I came?"

He pensively looked into her beautiful blue eyes and quietly responded, "Yes, Jenny, I know. How do you feel about that? There is an entire world out there you have not seen nor remember."

"Not sure, I guess I'm afraid of the unknown. I'd rather live up here for the rest of my life than take the chance of getting off the mountain."

"What if I were with you? Would you go then?"

Like a little girl, she sat there in silence and fiddled with her long braids. Finally, she answered, "I just don't know. I really never thought about leaving, but I think we need to get Kitty and Maud out of here. I have this awful feelin' it is wrong they're here."

"Why's that, Jenny?"

"It's been a long time, since any of the mountain men have brought young' uns up here; all of the "Golden Hairs" are grown women now and have families of their own, they don't seem to mind this way of life."

Frowning Louie asked, "Jenny, do you think it's fair they never had a choice to leave?"

"I suspect in the beginning, they all wanted to go back to their people but like me, I don't know if there is anybody I know that is still alive."

"But what if you did? What if there are still people out there that love you and want you to come home?"

Puzzled she glanced at Louie and softly touched his face, "But Louie Youngblood, this is my home."

Chapter 15
THE ROCK CAFÉ 1967

Judah Green loved living up on Black Fork Mountain with his daughters, but he had grown up in Waldron and missed the town. When he heard the rumors that Scott County Sheriff Hankins had retired, Judah Green was excited. Now he was free to visit Waldron any time that he pleased. Besides, he had also gotten wind that Ruby Lynn Franklin was running for Mayor of Waldron and her husband was running for the County Sheriff.

He decided today that he would visit the local Rock Café. He steered his beat-up pick truck into the parking lot and double-checked to make sure no cops were there eating before he made his way to the front door. He smirked as he walked inside and spied the old picture of John Wayne hanging on the brown paneled walls. His favorite spot to sit was in one of the hard booth seats admiring the black and white glossy picture of Marilyn Monroe on the wall. He especially liked the one of Elvis Presley. Back in his younger days, people always used to compare him to the famous singer from Memphis.

Judah Green did not like change. After the local politicians suggested putting in a 71 Bypass, he knew the idiots were all just plain stupid. Judah had studied the situation, and was aware that dumb maneuver would practically kill the traffic in the downtown area, this café would be forced to close down. But on the other hand, he liked the fact that not many young people frequented the café. They were loud smartasses, and they made fun of his hermit-like appearance. It irritated him that some of the rich brats got to go to college, and he had ended up in the damn military.

He ordered his usual western omelet and glass of sweet tea from his favorite waitress Jo Lynn. He had just settled back to read the free *Waldron Newspaper* she had placed on his table, compliments of the owner. The headlines on the front page jumped out at him **"The Franklin Team Wins by a Landslide!"**

He slammed down his paper and, much to his dismay, attracted the attention of one of the regular patrons, Freda Woodard. He grinned a toothless smile and, making no sense whatsoever, commented to her, "Omelet is hot, burned my mouth."

Through her black-framed glasses, Freda Woodard peered at the unshaven man with his uncombed hair. She frowned. He was not fooling her; she had witnessed his reaction to the headlines and took note of his anger.

While Green was eating, he devised a plan to put a thorn in the new mayor's side. He calmly finished eating his meal and left his cheap tip for Jo Lynn. Then he went to the nearest pay phone and dialed the number to the courthouse and left a message with the new Mayor's secretary, one she would never forget. Next, he went to his favorite spot where he had a good view of the Waldron Elementary School yard to wait.

Once before, he had already seen the little girl walking home alone after school and he had followed her. He figured that he could grab her without any problem. He was excited with anticipation of acquiring yet another "Golden Hair" and sticking it to the new mayor. He would have thought she would have crumbled like the social worker did when he got her kid but that damn Ruby Lynn Franklin, was now even more resilient.

Judah waited and watched as the little blond haired girl turned down West 2nd Street. At first, he stayed a few feet behind her checking each direction to make sure no one was behind him or coming toward him in the other lane. Following, he slowly turned down West 2nd Street when he saw the police cruiser in his rearview mirror. Judah cursed and passed the little girl. He kept on driving down the street. Once again, his big plans had been foiled by the damn police.

Chapter 16
THE MAYOR OF WALDRON

As she stood by her desk, looking up at the official statues of the state seal, Ruby Lynn pondered the true meaning of the emblem and its interpretation. At this moment, she was feeling inadequate and unprepared to carry out her duties. It had only been two years since she and Joe Bob had vowed they would never leave Arkansas until they found their missing daughter and Kitty Isaac.

Ironically, over a short period of time Ruby Lynn had entered the local political ring and was backed by the town folk who wanted answers to the girls' disappearance. She had a personal vendetta: she fought for stricter legislation, enforcement of child abduction laws, and the swift prosecution of the criminals who were accused of these horrifying acts.

This popular legislation had caused her career to skyrocket, placing her in a position to enter the political realm of her party. Some of her constituents were skeptical of her chances of winning the bid for mayor, but Ruby Lynn, an honest competitor, had proven to be a serious contender for the position. She had been elected by the residents of Scott County Arkansas as their first woman mayor.

She noted the eagle at the bottom of the state seal, holding a scroll in its beak, and hoped she could be as strong as the eagle. She was also the youngest sitting mayor of the state, what a massive task she had been given by her fellow citizens. Engrossed in thought, she absentmindedly slid her hand lovingly across the smooth wood grain of her Queen Anne desk, and her intercom buzzed.

In a businesslike manner, Darlene her secretary stated," Mayor, your team is here ready for the meeting. "Darlene hesitated, "That is, all but one."

Ruby Lynn frowned and immediately guessed which one of her esteemed team was running late. She said, "Thank you, please send them in."

She had formed a task force to deal with the kidnapping and personally selected a Who's Who of Law Enforcement to help her solve the crime.

Law enforcement had gotten a tip, regarding the whereabouts of her beloved Maud and Kitty. Ruby Lynn was nervous and hoped the lead would pan out because, after the girls' kidnapping her visions had disappeared, just like her sweet little daughter.

The first to enter her office was Sheriff Slade Garrett from Garland County. Ruby Lynn had met him a few times. She gathered, around these parts, he was somewhat of a football legend. Years later, his stocky physique still echoed his college quarterback days, and he was one hell of a cop.

Polk County Sheriff Brady Tolson was the next to arrive, Brady was tall and good-looking. As a kid, he had joined the local 4-H Club and had competed in the marksman competitions. Brady had gone on to win marksmanship contests all over the United States. He built a reputation for hitting his targets. At age eighteen, he became a Navy Seal and completed two tours in Korea as a sniper. He was about as good a tracker as he was a sniper.

Ruby Lynn stood impatiently waiting for the third and final member of the task force to arrive. She kept checking her watch, trying to remain calm and professional, but he really knew how to push her buttons. Sure, enough, her blood was boiling. The sheriff of Scott County, finally showed up, five minutes late.

She heard his deep voice and the distinctive sound of his cowboy boots running down the hallway and the giggles of her secretary. Joe Bob Franklin hurriedly tipped his Stetson hat to her and quickly sat down, stretching those damn long legs of his in her direction. He leaned over, dusted off his new cowboy boots, looked up at his wife, and grinned. A career change had been good for him. No matter how long they had been married, he still made her heart melt.

"Mayor, sorry I'm late, but, I got a last-minute call about the case."

She was wearing the red Antonio Melani suit he had bought her for Christmas. She had looked at the price tag and told him to return it, but he never did. It took all his will-power not to jump over her Queen Anne desk. She had bought it at a Flea Market and made him move it up all those dang stairs into her office. All he wanted to do at that moment was kiss her smack dab on those luscious red lips of hers. To hell what Slade and Brady thought, after all she was his wife.

Joe Bob and Ruby Lynn had been through so much the last two years. He could only hope this time they had a solid lead to find Maud and Kitty, still in Arkansas. Now that he was in law enforcement, he knew the chances of finding the girls was slim to none; but he and Ruby Lynn promised each other they would never give up hope of bringing the two girls home.

She took the maps out and spread them out on the top of her desk. She got a lump in her throat thinking, "In the beginning, this is how it all started, "remembering her beloved hometown of Cumberland Gap and the map she so desperately tried to find of Arkansas. She had singled out areas and marked various mountains in red. "This information is for your ears only and does not leave my office, my informant's life, may depend upon our discretion," she said.

Viewing the maps, Brady remarked, "Ruby Lynn, this is an awful lot of ground to cover; Black Fork and Rich Mountain alone, the terrain is rugged."

Slade frowned. "Besides, the weather right now is bitter cold up in most of the high peak areas."

Brady ran his hand through his thick gray hair and asked, "What do I tell my deputies? Why we are searching the mountains?"

Ruby Lynn looked at him in disbelief. "Brady, the only ones doing the searching is going to be us."

Brady blinked at her and said, "Shit, Ruby Lynn, no disrespect. I know we are good, but I don't know if we are that good."

Doing 180 degrees turn and agreeing with his fellow sheriff, Joe Bob interjected, "Honey, we all adore you, but this is a suicide mission. No good will come of this, even if we do sneak up on the perps. First, we have no idea which mountain to search first to find Maud or Kitty. Second, we do not know how many people are involved." She handed them a folded piece of her newly printed mayoral stationary with a picture of the state seal stamped at the top. The names of Steven Green and Louie Youngblood were printed on the sheet. Looking at the seal above her desk, she whispered, "May the Angel of Mercy guide and protect us to bring Maud, and Kitty home.

Chapter 17
BACK ON THE MOUNTAIN

The days were getting shorter. Dark had fallen upon the woods. Louie had shot a couple of rabbits that day, and Jenny had fixed a fine rabbit stew. The three of them had just sat down at the table. Maud giggled as she watched Pete circle his blanket five times before nestling down to take a little nap in front of the roaring fire. When the ritual was interrupted, Pete let out a yowl and headed straight for the door. Immediately, Louie jumped up from the table, grabbing the 30/30 from over the cook stove, and headed for the door.

"Stay back," he told Jenny. He slightly opened the door. Pete growled and slammed his nose into the door crack sticking his head out into the darkness. Then the wolf froze completely still. Louie opened the door wider, and to his disbelief he saw a young woman standing there shivering on the front porch. The oddest fact about her, was she looked like a younger version of Jenny. Stunned, Louie backed away from the door, watching Jenny's reaction to the woman, but it was if Jenny was unaware of the similarities.

Louie had begun to question the story Jenny's Mister had told her from the get-go. What if Jenny was just like the rest of the girls? What if she had been kidnapped from her family? And, even more bizarre, what if she had a sibling living here on the mountain? After two years, here, he had finally gained the mountain people's trust. He had started snooping around and finding out the truth; but for the meantime, he would lay low and not tell Jenny of his theories.

Not wanting to frighten the young woman, he softly said, "Jenny, I think someone wants to speak to you." Without thinking, Jenny grabbed her heaviest coat and her healing satchel and headed for the door. She left without a word to Louie or Maud about where she was going, and promptly shut the door behind her.

Jenny was not surprised to see one of the "Golden Hairs" at her door. The last time she had been down the mountain; she had calculated the weeks before one of the girls was going to give birth. It was especially cold that night, and she was appalled but not shocked to see that one of the men had sent this woman up the mountain, without a coat or even a blanket, instead of coming himself.

Once the two women walked into the clearing Jenny saw the dilapidated cabin. Upon entering the squalor was overpowering her senses. The rancid smell penetrated the small area and she automatically put her hand over her mouth to stop from gagging. It was dark inside and difficult to see. She needed additional light in order to work, and immediately scanned the room. The only light in the room emanated from the flames from the wood-burning fireplace. She breathed a sigh of relief when she established that the woman's Mister was nowhere to be found. She wondered if the woman who had come to fetch her came on her own accord. If that were the case, that was a gutsy move on her part. Jenny hated to think what would have happened to the poor woman if her Mister had come home and found her missing.

When the same woman took her by the hand and led her into the corner of the room, Jenny sucked in her breath. She was unprepared for the sight of all the blood spilled out onto the dirt floor. There, another young woman lay clutching her stillborn baby. The blank look in the young woman's eyes revealed that she knew her time was near, and that alongside her baby she, too, was going to die.

Sadly, Jenny understood there was no healing power on earth that would save the woman. Distraught, and with tears in her eyes, Jenny bent down and gently held her lovingly in her arms. The woman whimpered in pain. Jenny touched her fingers to the woman's lips and softly whispered, "Hush, now. Heaven's waitin' on you and your young'un. No reason to stay." The warmth from the fire dwindled before Jenny was able to release the young woman from her grasp. It was an odd feeling-none like she had ever felt before. Somehow, she hoped, she had made the woman's journey to the other side a bit easier.

Jenny's eyes had grown accustomed to the dim light. She saw the rest of the women trembling on the other side of the room in horror. Before Jenny left, she went outside, found a shovel, and buried the young woman and her child. She gathered some wood and stoked the fire so the remaining Golden Hairs would not freeze to death. She was eager to take her leave before their Mister came back home.

Jenny left in the dead of night. She was physically and emotionally exhausted when she began her trek up the mountainside, knowing full well the path was treacherous but she was anxious to get back home to her family. She was fatigued and struggling to stay awake. She stumbled, fell down, and was unable to stand back up.

Alone, Jenny sat there berating herself for being so careless. She knew better than to travel down the mountain without packing the appropriate overnight provisions. In her urgency to help, and focused on saving the Golden Hair, she had forgotten about her own welfare and now she was paying the price.

She wrapped her fur coat tightly around her body and scooted onto the rocks near a pine tree, pressing her back flush against the tree trunk and angling her body away from the brunt of the freezing winds. She was all too aware of the harsh elements, and of the hungry creatures roaming the woods. If the animals did not kill her, she estimated, she would not survive the brutal night temperatures. Eventually, she would freeze to death.

At first, she could not stop shaking. The bone-chilling wind wracked her body. Minutes faded into hours. She began drifting in and out of consciousness as her body grew numb and her hallucinations intensified.

She heard the howl of the wolf, and felt the odd sensation of the wet touch of an animal's nose against her face, nudging her frozen body with its warm fur. But she knew this was a dream. Pete was nowhere near here; he was with Louie and Maud back at their cabin.

In the dream, she saw Louie's blurry face in front of her and wished she had told him just how much she loved him. But it was too late. The mountain had other plans for her. Her eyes fluttered as she hypnotically watched flames circling into the night air. She imagined the strong touch of Louie's hands as he pulled her close, like lovers entwining their bodies into one.

The next morning, Jenny awoke disoriented and covered in animal pelts. She covered her head and dug deeper into the furs, relishing the cocoon of warmth engulfing her body. Briefly, she poked her head out and saw the smoke from the fire embers smoldering in the crudely dug fire pit. She smiled as she saw Pete lope up to her and screech to a halt when Louie called "Sit" to the excited animal.

Louie was carrying a bundle of firewood in his arms. He playfully nudged the wolf as he passed by him. He bent down and dropped the kindling into the pit. Satisfied with his work, he watched as the flames climbed higher and higher into the crisp morning air. Louie turned and carefully pulled the animal pelts back, trying not to disturb Jenny as he scooted his long body down deep into the bedding. First putting his long legs in and then pulling up the covering to his chin, he wrapped his body securely around Jenny's small frame. She snuggled close to him, loving his presence. She turned facing him and found his hands and gently entwined her fingers through his.

She could not wait any longer. She whispered in his ear, "I love you." He responded by boldly kissing her on the lips. She had no doubt that, for the rest of her life, Louie Youngblood would protect her from Black Fork Mountain.

Chapter 18
LEARNING THE HEALING WAYS

After Jenny's brush with death, Louie insisted she teach him everything she knew about the healing ways. He was constantly by her side, helping her tend to the sick and the injured. Jenny was impressed with what a quick study Louie had proved to be and how he was eager to help the mountain folk in any way he could do so.

A year had gone by and Louie still had no answer to why Jenny and one of the Golden Hairs favored each other. He had not said a word to her about his theory that she might have a sibling, or even parents, who had been searching for many years for her.

One day, after setting a mountain man's broken arm, Louie, Jenny and Maud were hiking back up the mountain trail, when Louie glanced over and noticed Jenny turning pale. Before he could catch her, she fainted. Panicking, he leaned down and quickly checked to see if she was hurt.

"Jenny, you okay?"

She opened her eyes and grinned up at him, touching one of his long braids, and said, "I hope our baby has your black hair."

At first, Louie did not grasp the meaning of what she had just told him. Then it dawned on him: she was carrying his child. Effortlessly, he lovingly scooped her up off the ground and cradled her in his arms the rest of the way to their cabin.

Once they arrived at the cabin, he told her in no uncertain terms that her days of doctoring were over for the next seven months. Louie would take up the healing tasks. Jenny was stubborn and balked at the idea, insisting that she was a mountain woman and capable of handling most anything.

A few months later, Jenny and Maud had tagged along with Louie and Pete on one of their hunting excursions. Jenny had rushed ahead of him, giving chase to a turkey hen, when he saw the water running down her leg. Her water had broken, she with a knowing look in her eye, she yelled, "Best get home or this young' un is goin' be born out here!"

Louie lifted her up in his arms and he, Maud and Pete sprinted up the hill toward the cabin. This was the first baby Louie had ever delivered, and he was a bit frightened. In between he and Jenny's crying tears of joy; he and his beloved Jenny, managed together to deliver a beautiful baby girl with dark hair and brown eyes and they named her "Naomi" after Louie's mother.

Chapter 19
THE THREAT

Immediately, the phone to the Waldron mayor's office started to ring off the hook. A legitimate threat had been made on the mayor's life. The caller insinuated that there would be an assassination attempt on Ruby Lynn's life. Due to the circumstances, Brady was convinced that somehow there had been a leak, but how could there be? The only people who knew about the task force had been sworn to secrecy. After the threat, protocol would have to be followed in order to protect the mayor, and that would mean too many people would need to be involved. The group had scheduled a recon trip to fly over the three mountains, but now they would have to forego the trip for today.

Once Ruby Lynn and Joe Bob arrived at her office in the Scott County Court House; they were surrounded. The governor of Arkansas had sent a security detail to watch over the new mayor. The team briefed her and Joe Bob about the threat on her life and how they had beefed up security around the county courthouse and the Franklin home in Waldron.

The mayor also had her secretary contact Slade and Brady to set up another meeting in her office the following morning.

That evening too wired up to retire, Ruby Lynn and Joe Bob had a nightcap in their formal den area. Ruby Lynn nestled into the tan wingback chair. She sipped on her hot toddy and lovingly gazed at her handsome husband as he settled into the matching chair beside her. She felt the heat of the fire warming her body. Her eyes wandered to the two small chandeliers adorning each side of the white fireplace mantel which dimly illuminated the room.

After all these years, and even after the threat, her husband had always been there by her side. She had felt safe, but now they were on a dangerous journey to find their missing daughter. Ruby Lynn's heart ached; she had tried to be strong. She had never shared her thoughts with her husband, but what if they finally found Maud and she had been dead all along? Ruby Lynn could not fathom the thought. She quickly tried to sweep it out of her mind. If Maud was really dead, there would be no more reason for Ruby Lynn to live. She thought back to how she had witnessed Joyce Isaac fall apart when Kitty was abducted. She had sworn to be strong for Joe Bob, but it was getting more difficult by the day.

Ruby Lynn tried not to be bitter. Larry Earl and Linda were both home, safe and sound with their parents. They had managed to somehow survive their ordeal with the kidnappers. Ruby Lynn was still puzzled why did the kidnappers grab Maud? It made a little sense when Joyce Isaac had explained the bad blood between her and the Green family, but if Youngblood and Green were the kidnappers, why did they take Maud?

Chapter 20
TIME TO GET DOWN TO BUSINESS

The Franklins awoke early in the morning and took Joe Bob's patrol car to the Scott County Court House. Before everyone arrived, Ruby Lynn had set up boards in her office with all the pertinent information on Kitty and Maud's case files. The group she had assembled would be concentrating on the possible localities: The Ouachita National Forest, Rich Mountain, and Black Fork Mountain.

Brady and Slade were the first ones to arrive; and all eyes turned to the mayor. Ruby Lynn had been sitting, examining all the data. Her muscles tightened when she opened the box containing Maud's personal effects that she had originally given the investigators. It did not seem possible it was only two years ago. Instead, it seemed like decades that her only child and Kitty Isaac had been missing. Ruby Lynn closed her eyes and methodically touched each item of her daughters. No one in the room dared to speak until Ruby Lynn had completely reviewed each piece of evidence.

Next, she closed her eyes and miraculously, the "Vision" ripped through her body. She could see the back of a lanky dark haired girl; Ruby Lynn reached out and touched the child and when she slowly turned; her green eyes glowed. Ruby Lynn cried out, "Maud! It's Momma!" as quickly as Ruby Lynn had envisioned her daughter, Maud was gone. Ruby Lynn tried to retrieve the moment. She would not awaken until she could see anything that would give a clue where Maud and Kitty were being held. Ruby Lynn heard the sound of a wolf cry, saw a woman with long blond hair and piercing blue eyes standing next to Maud, but there was no sign of Kitty.

Ruby Lynn did not want to wake up; she wanted to stay with the "Vision", this was the first time in two long years, she had been able to see her daughter but sadly, Ruby Lynn awoke. She stood up and briskly walked to the front of the room where the board stood. She closed her eyes once more then loudly slammed her hand down on an aerial shot of the mountain, Black Fork Mountain. Miraculously, her "Visions" had come back to her and without any hesitation in her voice, she said, "She is here."

Frantic, Joe Bob shouted, "What do you mean "She"? Oh, God! Ruby Lynn did you only see one girl?" Brady did not realize the meaning of what Joe Bob had just said until it was too late.

"Well, what are we waiting for? I've got all our gear in the squad car."

Ruby Lynn looked blankly at her husband and whimpered, "I only saw Maud, I did not see Kitty."

Much to her personal security detail's dismay, Ruby Lynn choose to ignore the threats to her life. She could sense that her team was on to something or someone. The threat on her life had only fueled her fire. Now that her "Visions" had once again returned, no one was going to stop her from finding her daughter and Kitty.

Chapter 21
GARAGE SALES

Several days before, as per his usual routine, Judah Green had cruised along Polk Road 44 and around Lake Mena looking for items he could use at his cabin or free clothes for his daughters before the garbage men came. When he would return from his weekly excursions to town with all his used free treasures, he had found that he was quite popular with not only his daughters, but the Golden Hairs and the mountain men. He was not really sure who disgusted him more: rich people, who had all that money and lived lavishly in their big houses and drove their fancy cars, or the cops; but today, he was concentrating on the rich.

There was a "Sold" sign on one of the houses on Polk Road 44. From the looks of it, the old owners were getting rid of stuff for the move. He noticed an old black typewriter. He got out, picked it up, and tossed it in the bed of his truck with the rest of the junk. The phone call he had made to the court house threatening the mayor's life was brilliant. On the way, back home, he came up with another plan to scare away the mayor from the Black Fork mountain. Self-assured as always, Judah tried to be a big man and impress his favorite Golden Hair. He showed her his new prize typewriter and bragged, "After I write this letter to the mayor, she won't dare set foot up here on our mountain."

He figured after the mayor got his letter, Ruby Lynn would get scared and back off. Once again, his ploy had backfired because as usual Judah had been too over-confident. To his chagrin, once she received the letter, she did not back off. Agitated, Judah heard through his sources that the threat had lit a fire under her ass.

The newspaper did a featured article how the mayor would not stop until she found the missing children. To make matters even worse, she and her husband had gone into the Cold Case files twenty years back and discovered there had been more kidnappings. The new sheriff had found a link: all the missing were white females, with blond hair and blue eyes all around the age of their daughter and Kitty.

Since Ruby Lynn had made the decision and chose to ignore his warning, if a fight was what she wanted; then by damn, Green would see to it that she was not disappointed. After the last death threat, did not work, he decided then and there that he would have to protect his own. He would gather all the mountain folks together, and he would personally go invite them to fight. If their mountains were going to be invaded by the law, they would all have to stand up and fight together as a united front to protect their way of life and their freedom.

He did not really care that the Elders had not given him permission to call for the meeting. His idea was that all clans from Ouachita and Rich Mountains would be joining the Black Fork Clan in two days' time.

Judah decided to personally visit each camp. When he did, he proclaimed that each of the mountain men were to bring their families, and together they would be prepared to fight. If the law came snooping, they would be armed and prepared to do battle, and as an added bonus Judah had organized an auction for the men to trade their Golden Hairs.

After Green, had returned from both mountains, he had requested a sit down with the Elders. Judah Green had never accepted the Indian and he was agitated Louie Youngblood would be present at the talk. The damn Elders had let Youngblood take over "The Healer" duties since his kid was born, and as the Healer of the clan, Louie Youngblood would be summoned to be present.

The first thing Louie noticed was how wild Judah Green appeared; his eyes darted quickly back and forth and his limbs were moving spastically while he spoke.

"I tell you they are comin' up here! Nothin' is goin' to stop that damn mayor!" Green screamed at the three elders.

His shrill, almost hysterical voice demanded, "We must fight, and the other clans agree!"

Louie watched as the three old men reacted to Green's paranoid rantings. Judah sputtered, "Our customs have grown lax."

The oldest of the three finally spoke, "Judah, we will not fight, unless forced to do so. We will talk to our brethren on the other mountains when they arrive and discuss the matter. Then and then only, will we come to a decision."

Louie pretended to look away when the "Elders" had not given Judah Green the answer he had expected, but Louie had seen the pure hatred in Green's eyes when he stomped out of the sit down. The Elders shared their concerns with Louie.

"Healer, we too, have ears and eyes everywhere, and we are aware the public is behind the Mayor of Waldron but we must wait."

Louie nodded he understood the stakes were high. He had heard rumblings from some of the mountain men that even the Governor of Arkansas was giving the mayor any resources she needed for her search for her child and for Kitty. Plus, now that after twenty years, the Cold Cases had been reopened, there was pressure from all the missing children's parents to find answers.

Louie was privy now to guarded information. The Elders always looked to each other for answers, they had lived in peace for the last twenty years; but Judah Green had changed all that when he had his nephew and Louie bring the two girls up the mountain. Life as the mountain men had known it was going to change drastically.

After hearing of Green's crazy plan, Louie felt he had no other choice. If he did not do something, people were going to get killed. He was not going to take the chance of something happening to his baby, Jenny, Maud or Kitty.

Life on the mountain had been good to Louie Youngblood. There was no changing the fact that he was a fugitive from the law. If he stuck to this dangerous course of action, he would lose everything. He had been blessed with the love of a good woman and a child. It had only been two years, but he had never forgotten his promise. He would protect Jenny from Black Fork Mountain. He would sacrifice his life for her and their child. Now it was time to make good on his promise. He loved Jenny with every breath in his body, but he had to be honest with her. Once he got back to the cabin, he would have to inform her of his plan.

Louie saw Jenny outside cradling Naomi while watching Pete and Maud playing together. She lovingly greeted him. He tried to smile, but she could see the tension in his body as he approached. "Husband, did it not go well with the council?" she asked. When he did not respond, she carefully handed Naomi to Maud, "Maud, please take the baby inside for her feedin'." Maud looked down at the babe in her arms and smiled. She had grown close to her new family but she still had an ache in her heart for her Momma and Papa.

Taking Jenny's hand, Louie guided her under the big pine tree where he had first seen her two years ago. He wished deep down inside the circumstances of their lives had been different somehow and would never change. He only had a small window to report to the authorities what was about to go down on the mountain. Louie only hoped, for everyone's sake, that before they threw him in jail and locked him up for the rest of his life, or killed him, that they would listen to his vital information.

High above their heads, the snow clouds were starting to form. Jenny pulled her fur coat tighter as she listened carefully to his story.

"Jenny, it may not have been right but I wrote down what happened to each of the Golden Hairs.

Her blue eyes grew large as he took a deep breath and carefully proceeded onward, "I hid the list in our cabin but now it is time to share my findings and to tell you the truth."

Jenny had no idea he had been documenting each girl's story, including her own.

"I am convinced that you had two sisters when you came here. You were around three then, one of your sisters was two and the other would have been around one".

Her eyes started to glisten with tears and she whispered, "The younger one died in childbirth, didn't she?"

Startled Louie's hand began to tremble, "How did you know?"

"The night she died, I held her in my arms and it was like lookin' into my own eyes."

Louie held her tightly in his arms and kissed away her tears, "Jenny, I think your other sister may be alive and still here on the mountain. You must find her; she does not know about you."

"Why are you tellin' me all this?" She could hear the tremor in her own voice. She searched his brown eyes. She did not need for him to answer, her heart shattered in her chest and her body became overcome with pain, "Oh, God. You are leavin."

The only solace to Louie's departure was he felt better knowing that, once he was no longer in Jenny's life, somewhere out there she, the baby and her sister must have a family searching for them who loved and missed them.

With a heavy heart, Louie Youngblood packed his satchel and prepared Maud for the journey. He prayed the mask of darkness would help protect them on their trek down Black Fork Mountain. Helplessly sobbing, Jenny clung to him, begging him not to leave, but he knew it was finally time to go. He kissed her and walked out the door. Maud was anxious to get going and was impatiently waiting on the trail.

Not looking back, he smiled as he pictured Jenny as he had first seen her, standing outside with her long hair gently blowing in the breeze and her skirt wrapping playfully around her ankles. Louie Youngblood refused to live life without her and Naomi; he would rather die. But first he had to ensure their safety, and return the two girls to civilization, so going to the authorities was his only choice. But the task of taking Kitty away from Judah Green would more than likely prove to be difficult.

As Louie and Maud quickly descended the mountain, Ruby Lynn and the first reconnaissance team were organizing the climb up the mountain. The group was on edge and highly charged after their first attempt had been foiled by some nut job and his threats. This time, they decided not to fly; all of the parties had driven to the Pope County Sheriff's station. It was nearly 4:00 p.m., and Slade felt it was too late to journey up the mountain. Ruby Lynn insisted, since they all were there, that a small reconnaissance mission could not hurt. Pressed by her decision and her rank, Blade divided the group into three separate search parties. Brady would take the south side of the mountain; Slade would take the west side of the mountain; and Joe Bob and Ruby Lynn would take the east side.

Before departing, Joe Bob firmly stated, "You have one hour to get in and take a look around, and then get the hell out. If you see anything suspicious, use your cameras and take pictures, but whatever you do, don't let anyone see you. Are we all clear on that last point?" The group nodded their heads in agreement. Dressed in camouflage, each grabbed their backpacks and solemnly prepared to cover the area assigned to each one. Joe Bob estimated that one hour would be sufficient time to test the waters and see how much ground each team could cover within the designated time span. He worried the hike might be too strenuous for Ruby Lynn, but she would not stay behind; she insisted on coming along and seeing this through to the end.

As Joe Bob slung his rifle over his shoulder, Slade was quick to inquire, "That one of those Remington 700 models?" Joe Bob patted the rifle. "Yeah, and got me a Redfield scope with it for a steal."

Slade proudly showed Joe Bob his new weapon. "Got my 300 Winchester Mag."

Joe Bob nodded. "See you got the heavy barrel to boot."

Ruby Lynn interrupted, holding her rifle, "Still like my old Winchester carbine."

Double checking the chamber of his police-issued .357 Magnum, Brady chuckled, "Nothin' wrong with that."

The small talk seemed to help calm their nerves. Each shooter was intensely aware of how risky this recon mission might be. Each silently prayed they would not be forced to shoot. But if forced to shoot, each had been trained to kill.

The climb up the mountain was steep and extremely physically challenging, even for the trained professionals. Joe Bob noticed Ruby Lynn was lagging behind, so he slowed his pace. Even though he felt the wind turn cooler, he could not pull the earflaps of his fur lined cap over his ears, for he was alert for the faintest sounds.

They had hiked to the first bluff when Joe Bob got a whiff of smoke. Stopping, he threw his fist in the air. Without a word, Ruby Lynn immediately halted. Joe Bob pointed into the sky and Ruby Lynn nodded when she saw the smoke whirling into the atmosphere.

Joe Bob checked his watch. They only had fifteen minutes left before they were due back at base camp at the edge of the mountain. He was torn whether to turn back now or proceed onward. His gut told him they were onto something and not to turn back. Promptly, he motioned for Ruby Lynn to hit the ground, and he climbed on his belly to the edge of the bluff and pulled out his binoculars. He gestured for Ruby Lynn to crawl to his position near the edge. Ruby Lynn stealthily came crawling up to the ledge and lay next to him.

Joe Bob could hear Ruby Lynn's heavy breathing. She was trying hard to slow it down. She was good with a gun and this was not her first kill. She knew if she had to discharge her weapon like before when she had shot the sheriff back home, she would need to remain calm, cool and collected.

Under the circumstances, Joe Bob was glad his wife was with him. She never let him forget she was born up in the Appalachian Mountains and grew up dirt poor, and she made no bones about being raised with a rifle in her hand. She never ceased to amaze him with her innate skills as a hunter and tracker. The underbrush and the dense overgrowth of the woods made it difficult to locate where the smoke had actually originated. He wondered if it was just a small forest fire. But at closer view, through the thick trees, he had finally been able to locate a dilapidated cabin.

Ruby Lynn tapped him on his arm and motioned in another direction. She had seen something else. She pointed to a small wooden structure. Joe Bob quickly pulled his Remington from its sheath and expertly adjusted the magnification on his scope, placing the butt of the weapon flush into his shoulder. He saw the lean-to and surmised it was an outhouse.

Joe Bob had zoomed his sights onto the small building when the door slowly opened and out popped the head of a young girl. She was barefoot, and hesitated before she stepped out, and then scampered toward the cabin. A dog started barking and came running toward her and jumped up, knocking her down; she found a stick in the dirt and threw the stick high in the air.

Joe Bob saw an unkempt looking man come bursting out of the cabin. He jerked the young girl by the hair and threw her like a ragdoll against the outside wall of the cabin. She crawled away, kicking at him, but she was no match against his large build. He followed her and roughly grabbed her and started ripping off her clothes.

Instinct kicked in, and Joe Bob took a breath and then slowly released it and squeezed gently on the trigger of his high-powered rifle. He had to make his shot count, he could not miss his target of the man. Seeing the little girl's face, Joe Bob had no doubt in his mind the little girl was Kitty Isaac.

The sound of the one shot echoed through the trees as the bullet hit its mark. The man instantly gazed through the trees and up in the direction of the bluff, and fell cumbersomely over on top of Kitty, dead. She began to scream, frantically trying to dislodge the dead body off of her small frame. Joe Bob jumped up and started racing down the bluff, slipping and sliding on the harsh terrain, with Ruby Lynn following fast behind him. Joe Bob was afraid, they only had seconds to respond before someone would come to investigate. Not wanting her hopes up he was waiting to tell Ruby Lynn they had found Kitty, but as yet, there was no sign of Maud.

Louie Youngblood had only made it halfway down the mountain when he heard the sound of an unfamiliar gunshot. Louie started to panic. He knew none of the men in the clan owned such a high-powered rifle, and strangers had to be among them. He listened, singling out the direction. The shot echoed, and he started running as fast as he could toward the sound with Maud trailing after him.

Louie wished with all his might that he was the only one who had detected the difference in the sound; he dreaded the outcome if he were too late. Reassured, he realized that if others had heard the shot, surely by now, they would have sounded the alarm. As of this moment, he was the only person on the mountain who could save the stranger who had discharged the weapon.

Joe Bob looked up and the sun was setting behind what appeared to be snow clouds. His pulse raced. Joe Bob could only speculate, but at this rate, they would be in unfamiliar territory, trying to find their way out in the dark. He and Ruby Lynn came to the clearing by the cabin and stopped. Neither one of them moved. When the group had started the recon mission; they had only anticipated or hoped of rescuing two children. Joe Bob was astounded when three more girls in their teens had come out of the dwelling and were helping pull the dead man's body off Kitty.

Straightaway, Ruby Lynn laid her rifle down in the thick brush and silently crept nearer to the girls. The older girl spit and kicked the man's dead body and the younger girls followed her lead. When the youngest girl turned around, Ruby Lynn saw that, the child was Kitty.

Fortunately, at first the girls had not noticed Ruby Lynn entering their property. Startled and afraid, the teenagers stood deathly still as they watched Ruby Lynn raise her hands in the air, showing them she was unarmed. Ruby Lynn calmly stepped toward the group. She directed her attention to Kitty, who looked dazed but not as filthy as the other three girls.

When the older girl stepped forward, looking at Ruby Lynn, and bravely asked, "Was it you who killed that Mister?"

Joe Bob did not move, but answered, "No, that would be me," and pointed to his badge. "I am a Sheriff."

Ruby Lynn bent down on one knee and whispered, "Kitty, it's me, the Gypsy."

She still had not spoken, her eyes filled with tears as she ran toward Ruby Lynn, Ruby Lynn took her into her arms and held her tightly.

"You're safe now."

The older girl wiped her hands on her filthy skirt and bravely rushed up to Joe Bob and extended her hand for him to shake. She continued, "Our daddy asked him to be watchin' us while he was away. When he finds out what that piece of shit tried to do to us, he'll be glad that you killed him."

Joe Bob frowned. "When are you expectin' your daddy back?"

She scratched her ratty hair and said, "Don't rightly know. Sometimes he's gone for days."

Worried, Ruby Lynn looked at the three girls and handed them a photograph of Maud and said," Have you seen this girl?"

The older girl took the photo of Maud and shook her head, "Don't recognize her, but our daddy don't let us mingle much with the "Golden Hairs." Ruby Lynn held Kitty even closer to her body but Kitty had still not spoken.

Joe Bob quizzed the older girl, "Golden Hairs?"

"Yes, sir. We don't get to see em' much but heard tell there are several livin' up here with their Misters, like her. The older girl pointed directly to Kitty as if to explain what she was talking about.

"I'm not sure I follow what you are talking about?" So, your father brought you here to live?"

The older girl responded, "Yes, sir." Then she looked down at the body, "We got to bury him; otherwise, the varmints will smell him rotting," Resolutely, almost mechanically she retrieved an old shovel with a broken wooden handle leaning up against the outhouse. She quickly handed Joe Bob the shovel and urged, "Best bury him far from the cabin."

By the time Joe Bob finished digging the shallow grave, it was nearly dark outside. Ruby Lynn was visibly shaken; they had not found Maud. If Maud were still alive, she only prayed she was still here, on Black Fork Mountain and whoever kidnapped her had not disappeared with her daughter.

Joe Bob was acutely aware that the rescue party was scheduled to have left over thirty minutes ago for base camp. He, like Ruby Lynn, was afraid if Maud was here on the mountain, whomever had her would panic. No telling what would happen to her. Joe Bob also knew, for Kitty's sake, they must leave. Since they no longer had the light of day, the most difficult part of their journey would be to attempting to retrace their steps.

She, Kitty and Joe Bob were about to leave when Ruby Lynn saw a dark shadow, deep in the woods. She strained her eyes and saw his silhouette, standing tall. Shocked, she watched the wind playfully catching his long braids lying on his chest. In recognition of a ghost from her past, Ruby Lynn's body began to shake all over.

As the figure came closer into view, Louie held his weapon high in the air, with both hands, reaching over his head. His face was still as handsome as she had remembered. He strode up to the group with purpose. She saw his taut thigh muscles and his firmly-set jaw. She was speechless; Louie Youngblood was alive and on Black Fork Mountain.

Louie Youngblood bravely moved toward the cabin. The older girl recognized him and excitedly ran toward him. She called out, "Don't shoot! It's the Healer!"

Concerned, Louie asked her, "I heard the shot, are any of you hurt?"

With hatred in her voice, the older girl angrily replied, "Nope, not now. That fella shot that piece if shit who has been stayin' here while our daddy was gone."

As Louie came a few feet closer, Joe Bob aimed his rifle in his direction. With mixed emotions, Ruby Lynn touched the barrel of her husband's rifle, "It's Louie Youngblood."

Joe Bob out of pure spite upon hearing his name, wanted to shoot the bastard but refrained in case Youngblood knew the whereabouts of his Maud.

Coming closer to her, Louie Youngblood called out, "Ruby Lynn Franklin?"

Ruby Lynn's voice was almost a whisper as she responded, "Yes?"

He said, "I heard the shot, that is why I am here." He continued, "But first, these are names of all the Golden Hairs that are missing." He took her hand in his and gave her the folded piece of paper and sent Greens' daughters back inside the cabin. He did not want them privy to the information he was about to divulge and he sure as hell did not want the girls to know his next move.

Confused, she asked, "Golden Hairs?"

When he turned and she thought he was leaving, but instead he called, "Maud, it's safe to come out!"

Ruby Lynn's knees felt weak. She tightly gripped Joe Bob's arm for support and began uncontrollably sobbing. The shadowy figure slowly came out from where she had been hiding. Once, Maud recognized her mother, she screamed," Momma! Papa!" and Maud started running toward her parents. Ruby Lynn dropped to her knees, opening her arms toward her daughter.

"Oh, my God! Oh, thank God! You're alive!" Ruby Lynn cried.

Joe Bob's arms encircled them, his baby girl had been found.

"We got to get going," Louie stated.

"Why should we trust you?" Joe Bob asked.

"I'm your only chance to get Kitty and Maud off this mountain alive."

Holding on to Maud tightly, Ruby Lynn looked at her husband and nodded, "It's nearly dark and we need to get to safety. Someone is bound to have heard that shot."

Attuned to the sights and sounds of the woods, Louie's body swiftly wove in and out of the dense forest. Joe Bob, Ruby Lynn, Maud and Kitty were behind him, closely tracing each of his steps.

Louie demanded, "We've got to pick up our pace."

Even though Joe Bob still did not trust Louie Youngblood, he grasped the severity of their situation. He knew none of them would make it out of the woods alive without Youngblood's help, and Joe Bob at least owed him that.

Louie pointed into the sky and stopped. He could see the street lights illuminating the streets of downtown Mena. He had completed his task and felt an urgent need to get back to Jenny and his child. But he had made the decision to turn himself into the police for the crimes he had committed with Steve Green, and he was man enough to accept whatever punishment he was given.

Ruby Lynn stopped to catch her breath and said, "Joe Bob, what do we do now?"

Louie Youngblood started to walk into the street light when Ruby Lynn reached for his arm. He turned and she looked into his eyes and hissed, "How could you do this to us? How could you have taken Maud?"

Before Louie could answer Joe Bob whispered, "We don't have time for this now, but make no doubt about it, I will be back to arrest you."

Solemnly, Louie nodded and he answered, "There is something else you need to know. In two days' time, all the men who have "Golden Hairs" are coming up on the mountain."

Louie turned and started to run back toward the mountain. Joe Bob grimaced, "Golden Hairs?"

Over his shoulder, Louie yelled, "They are girls who were kidnapped and hidden up here. Be careful, some of the law is dirty around here."

Joe Bob did not want to take any chances. He saw Ruby Lynn and the girls wandering toward the street light and he took off chasing after them, catching his wife by her sleeve of her coat before she could make it out into the open view of the street. He clasped her arm and urged her to stop.

Confused and a bit disoriented, she stopped, and Joe Bob took her into his arms and held her. Maud gazed up and smiled at her father, "Daddy" was all he needed to hear from her, he had his little Maud back. Now it was time for him to get her home. Kitty was still not talking and he started to worry if she had gone into shock.

Suddenly, the beams from the spotlight caught Joe Bob's attention as it bounced off the vacant old buildings in the downtown area. The cruiser was stopping at all the side streets, and shining the spot light in the dark alleys. Joe Bob whispered, "Duck down."

Puzzled at his request, Ruby Lynn was about to say something when he put his finger gently to her lips to silence her. They huddled silently together in the darkness. Joe Bob quietly took out the keys to his patrol car. After Louie's warning, Joe Bob was in a quandary. Who in law enforcement could he trust? Since they were in Polk County, he did not want to alert Brady because the snitch was more than likely in his department or on the Mena Police Force. He, Ruby Lynn, Maud and Kitty began moving in and out of the back alleys of the buildings, trying to avoid the patrol unit and Joe Bob wished this would all be over.

It was freezing outside. Ruby Lynn looked down. Kitty's lips were turning blue and her teeth had started to chatter. Ruby Lynn watched as snowflakes fell on Kitty's bare head.

Ruby Lynn grimaced as the snow started sticking on to her camo jacket. She had lived in or near mountains all her life. When the roads started to freeze with snow and ice, traveling in the curvy remote area was near impossible. One wrong turn and your vehicle could careen down an embankment, and the likelihood of being found was nearly impossible, especially if there came a whiteout and the visibility was near zero. She glanced over at Kitty, who still had that blank look on her face. Ruby Lynn started to panic.

Disappointed, he had not seen a soul. Slade had climbed up the mountain and back within the hours' time line, and had gone back to the sheriff's office to wait for the rest of the search party. He had a nagging feeling, something was just not quite right. Joe Bob had been adamant about the time frame, but he and Ruby Lynn were still not back. Slade jumped when Brady walked into the station. He too, had made it down the mountain, safe and sound. Slade's mood changed drastically as he looked at the clock on the wall. He chided, "We'd better get to our squad cars, something ain't right." Worried, Brady frowned. "They're predictin' a heavy snowfall here tonight. They ain't equipped to stay the night out there."

Before they had headed up the mountain, the three lawmen had devised a secret channel on their police radios for communications, but as Slade and Brady anxiously waited in their patrol cars, all communications were eerily quiet.

Chapter 22
THE SNOW STORM

The snowflakes fell onto Judah Green's cracked front windshield, and he madly swiped at the frost accumulated on the glass. He cursed at his damn defroster, which was not working. Judah Green had just finished putting the final touches to his meeting with the other men from Rich Mountain, and he needed to get back to Black Fork Mountain as soon as possible to check on his girls. He thought back and commended himself on how he had singlehandedly organized the event. Absent-mindedly, he picked at the loose threads that sprang from the worn-out upholstery of his truck bench seat and grabbed the bottle of Wild Turkey. He took a swig from the bottle and lit a Green Camel cigarette.

He surmised that by the time he gathered all the folks together, they would oust the Elders and make him the head honcho. Celebrating his new fame, he had acquired, he had not made up his mind what would be his new title. But he definitely felt he had earned the honor resembling a person of royalty, like King or Magistrate or something along those lines.

Feeling the effects of the alcohol warming him up inside, he began to get tired of driving and yearned for the companionship of one of the Golden Hairs, but that good loving would have to wait. He was famished, so instead of hiding his truck in his usual spot, he decided to pull onto 601 on US 71, and drive to Mena and get something to eat. Judah was lost in thought and not paying attention to the road when his truck fishtailed and slid to the right, nearly careening into a ditch.

He grimaced, "That was too damn close."

Thank goodness, without too much trouble he had been able to maneuver into the parking lot of a restaurant nearby. He cursed when he saw a local police car in the lot. He hated the law and seeing them made him want to puke. His appetite was ruined, and he slowly turned his truck around and left the parking lot. Angrily, he noted that the roads had gotten slicker; it was going to be slow going as he attempted to make his way back home toward Black Fork Mountain.

Chapter 23
PASSING IN THE NIGHT

Joe Bob quickly got on the police radio in the car and switched on to the one channel he, Slade and Brady had agreed to use. Joe Bob tried to stay calm, but Ruby Lynn could detect the edge in his voice. "Slade, things are going to hell in a hand basket here. I need backup now."

Alarmed, Slade answered, "Where?"

"We are at the intersection of Magnolia and $2^{nd.}$ We got them out. They're with us," Joe Bob replied.

"Copy that. We are on our way." Slade assured.

Joe Bob suspiciously looked around. Into the microphone he added, "Come in silent." The two patrol cars sped down the streets of Mena without lights and sirens until they came to Magnolia and 2nd, where they saw the Scott County Sheriff's patrol car parked without any headlights on. Joe Bob jumped out of the car and met Slade's vehicle.

Joe Bob stammered, "I think, we've been made by a patrol car."

Alarmed, Slade countered, "Which force?"

Joe Bob grimaced, "Didn't get a close look but I think it was M.P.D."

Slade cursed, "Shit! We need to get goin' then and pronto, how are the girls?"

Joe Bob shook his head, "Maud seems okay, but Kitty went through hell out there."

Slade and Joe Bob quickly climbed back into their patrol units.

Once back in the patrol unit, Joe Bob looked back at Kitty and said, "We need to contact the Isaacs as soon as possible."

Ruby Lynn knew the look on his face all too well. She too, was concerned that Kitty was in bad shape and said, "I understand."

The only problem was that Joe Bob did not want a police sent to the Isaac house. With his new knowledge of the leak in law enforcement, he did not need for anyone to know that they had rescued the two missing children. In the midst of the snow storm, the three patrol cars rolled out of town, trusting that no one was aware of the precious cargo they carried with them.

Judah Green felt as if he had been on the road forever when the three patrol cars passed him at high speeds. He got a glimpse of the woman in the front seat.

He screamed, "Shit! Shit! Shit! That bitch!"

He pulled over on the side of the road and started slamming his head against the steering wheel. He did not stop until the blood started spilling from his open cut. It seemed like the only luck today he was having was bad luck; he would personally have to do something about the damn mayor.

"What in the hell was the mayor doing here?"

Let her bring out her big guns, and let's just see who is the last man standing! Even though he had not been originally from the mountain, he valued the mountain folk's way of life. After all, they had been hidden up in the mountains ever since the Great Depression. Judah knew no one was going stop their way of life. The men would fight to the death because no one was going to take away their Golden Hairs. Green looked in the rearview mirror and smeared the blood from his forehead.

Chapter 24
THE BARRICADE

Ruby Lynn advised the team that once they arrived at the hospital, someone needed to call Freda in Waldron, and tell her to go get Kitty's parents and bring them to Hot Springs. Joe Bob agreed to her plan; no one would suspect anything was amiss if their former nanny came calling on the couple.

They were taking the girls to St. Vincent's in Hot Springs where the Garland County Sheriff's Department could personally guarantee their safety. If the situation changed, someone would radio Slade, and he would have a backup plan in place.

This plan would guarantee that they would have three patrol units, from Scott, Polk and Garland counties, traveling together and escorting them. Slade had already cleared with Joe Bob that one of his Deputy Sheriff's would be armed and waiting at the hospital emergency entrance for their arrival. After setting up all the details once there in Hot Springs, Ruby Lynn would make the call up to the state capitol and inform the governor of their whereabouts putting the plan into motion.

Joe Bob made no bones about it to Ruby Lynn, "The trip to Hot Springs is going to be a dangerous one. There was a reason the locals dubbed these parts of the drive from Mena to Hot Springs 'Snake Mountain'. The sharp twists and turns are difficult to navigate in excellent weather conditions, and we are going to be fighting a snow storm, which makes the trip even more hazardous. Ruby Lynn, the Ouachita National Forest mountains are no joke."

Concerned, Ruby Lynn adjusted the two girls' safety belts a bit more tightly and coaxed, "Hold on girls, we will be there soon".

Kitty still sat there tightly clutching Ruby Lynn's hand and did not say a word. Maud looked at Kitty and said, "Don't worry, Kitty. My Daddy will get us there, and you will get to see your folks."

Joe Bob paused, thinking how different this drive in inclement weather would be for him. Most of the time, his main duties in snow and ice were to transport doctors and nurses for their shifts to and from the hospital. Joe Bob had cranked the heater on full blast and he was starting to sweat. He glanced into his rearview mirror. Maud and Ruby Lynn had Kitty sitting in between them. All three were still shivering. He could only hope they had not been exposed too long in the outdoor elements; the worst-case scenario was a case of hypothermia. He knew the little girls were more at risk than Ruby Lynn. Ruby Lynn had tried to keep the girls warm, but both girls had been through so much already. Kitty didn't even have a parka to cover her head. From his first aid courses at the academy, he had learned that a large amount of body heat is lost through the head.

Joe Bob was concentrating on the obvious task--getting them all safely to the hospital. He was at a loss and perplexed at the second obstacle: he had no idea how he could secretly organize law enforcement and go undetected back to the Black Fork Mountain. Ruby Lynn and her task force had made a discovery; there were more kidnap victims being held against their will on not only Black Fork but on the other two mountains. God only knew if they would be there in time to find out where the gathering was being held. And if by chance they did find them, they had no clue how much fire power they would need for a safe rescue.

The rescue team would be going in blind, they did not have any statistics on how many what Youngblood called Golden Hairs were up on Rich or in the Ouachita's. It was like playing dominoes; if one domino fell, the rest would come crashing down. Once the kidnap victims were extracted, law enforcement would have to orchestrate transportation and set up medical assistance somewhere on site. If there was an altercation, all the offenders would be taken to the nearest prison facility down in Texarkana. And if that wasn't bad enough, he did not have a clue how many people were involved in the travesty.

Law enforcement would have only one shot; the key would be to get in there undetected, to keep from getting any law enforcement officers killed and protect the kidnap victims at the same time. No matter how well the operation was planned and organized, he could not calculate the unknown variables. He was deathly afraid that this insurmountable task was going to get people killed.

He was on autopilot as he drove this familiar stretch of highway, which he knew like the back of his hand. They would be approaching the Polk and Garland County lines within minutes. He was all too acquainted with these elevations, and he was not surprised that the snow was not letting up.

Joe Bob gritted his teeth and pressed down on the gas pedal. When he caught a glimpse of the blue and white lights flashing up ahead, the snow was coming down so heavily, he could barely see Slade and Brady's headlights behind him. He had not heard any chatter on the police radio since they drove onto U.S. 70. and they were basically on their own. He looked at the speedometer and started slowing down his police cruiser. But he changed his mind when he got closer and saw several men standing in front of a road block with weapons drawn. Somehow word had gotten out of their reconnaissance mission, but he was puzzled as to who was the leak and where.

Joe Bob yelled, "Get down! Put your heads down! "

Ruby Lynn sprang into action, unbuckled Kitty and Maud and shoved them to the floorboard. Ruby Lynn grabbed her Winchester from off the top of the backseat window. She checked the chamber and cocked the weapon, then rolled down the back-seat passenger window, sticking the gun barrel menacingly outside.

Joe Bob commanded, "We're going through! Hold on! Ruby Lynn, fire if you can get a shot off." With all his might, he slammed his foot down on the accelerator pedal, flush with the floorboard; the cruiser's engine responded with an angry groan, testing the limits of the eight cylinders grinding under the hood. The cruiser shot forward, forcing the men to either stand their ground or run for cover. The majority dove wildly into the nearby ditches for safety. By charging the barricade, Joe Bob had caught them off guard, but several were able to get off a shot.

Ruby Lynn could hear the muffled sound of the bullets pelting the outside of the patrol car. Not flinching, Ruby Lynn expertly fired into the crowd. As the men parted, Slade and Brady sped past them, following closely behind the Scott County patrol car and its driver.

Joe Bob figured they had sustained some exterior damage in the confrontation, but that was to be expected. Kitty had tears rolling down her face as she and Maud crawled off the floor board and onto the back seat.

Joe Bob glanced in Ruby Lynn's direction and saw her face turning deathly pale. Ruby Lynn whispered "I'm hit," and touched her left side.

Keeping his wits about him, Joe Bob instructed, "Honey, how bad it is?"

Her hands were shaking as she inspected the wound. "Oh! God, Joe Bob! Oh, God!" her voice quivered.

Joe Bob's heart was beating fast. "Maud, there is a first aid kit under my seat; I will tell you what to do." She followed his instructions, and applied pressure to her mother's gunshot wound.

Joe Bob shouted, "Ruby Lynn, you hold on, we are almost there." Right away, he switched on his running lights and his siren. Surprised, Slade and Brady answered the call and began following in hot pursuit; the mission was no longer silent. The emergency lights cut through the snow and the sirens wailed as all three police vehicles topped speeds of over one hundred miles per hour.

Expertly, Joe Bob spun the cruiser racing toward St. Vincent's Hospital. Brady did not know who was hurt, but he radioed ahead for his deputy to have emergency personnel and medical staff standing by to administer to the injured. Still, no one at the hospital was to be made aware that the mayor's entourage was coming in hot and involved in a search and rescue operation.

Joe Bob jumped from his patrol car and followed the gurney carrying Ruby Lynn into the Emergency Room. Before anyone could see the girls, Slade and Brady covered Maud and Kitty's heads with their patrol jackets and whisked them inside. Instantly, the Garland County Sheriff's Deputy drew his weapon and placed his body protectively in front of the Emergency Room door.

Chapter 25
AT THE HOSPITAL

In a split second, the Garland County Sheriff's Deputy was no longer standing alone at his post. Sheriff Brady Tolson from Polk County, as well as his own Sheriff, Slade Garrett had returned and all joined him, making a human barricade lining the entrance to the hospital. No one would be allowed in and no one would be allowed out.

In the cold, not moving for hours, the three stood guarding the mayor and her mysterious charges. That wing of the hospital had been locked down, and security procedures were activated. Under the veil of secrecy, Joe Bob had called Ruby Lynn's own private Arkansas State Police detail, and reinforcements were on their way from Waldron to Hot Springs. Upon the state troopers' arrival, Slade and Brady were finally able to breathe a sigh of relief; reinforcements had arrived and everyone was safe.

Ruby Lynn had only sustained a flesh wound and did not even need stitches. Joe Bob knew his wife and nothing was going to keep her from completing her mission; she complained of only being a little sore. The next thing he knew she had dressed and had gotten out of bed, checking on their daughter and Kitty.

Maud and Kitty had also been rushed into the Emergency Room and each was seen by the doctors on duty. Maud was in excellent condition but the staff was extremely concerned about Kitty's condition. She was malnourished and was teetering on developing a case of pneumonia.

At dawn, Joe Bob and Ruby were gathered around Maud's hospital bed when they noticed the light shining through the closed blinds. Ruby Lynn peeked through the blinds. The snow and ice had begun to melt; this was typical of the unpredictable weather in Arkansas.

The outside doors were still being manned by armed guards when Ruby Lynn heard a ruckus. The human barricade parted and the door opened. Freda Woodard importantly burst into the hospital with Kitty's parents. The Joyce and Jack Isaac were nervous and anxious to see their daughter, so right away they were shown to her private hospital room. The room was under a high security warning, and armed guards were stationed outside. Joe Bob was impressed; his wife, the mayor, was barking orders at anyone within ear shot. The small team of three law enforcement officers had now been tripled in size, and per her orders, the Arkansas State Police would help orchestrate the search and rescue up on Black Fork Mountain.

The hospital staff had graciously designated a meeting room for the mayor and her police detail to wait; but instead they made excellent use of the facility and started mapping out strategies for which areas and duties each would be responsible. The top priority on the list, however, was executing the safe removal of the kidnap victims. Ruby Lynn stressed the less casualties the better. After the attack at the Polk and Garland County lines, her task force was one hundred percent sure there was a leak in local law enforcement. Looking back on the incident, the only way anyone could have known what was going on was that Joe Bob and the others had to have been seen in Mena by whomever was driving the patrol car at that time.

Brady's job was to phone the Chief of Police in Mena and narrow down who was on duty that night. Brady had to proceed with caution; this was going be a sticky situation. The task force was going on a hunch, and they did not have proof. Brady was deeply aware of the damage to the department and to the officer if an accusation of that scale was found to be false. The legal fallout alone could cost him and others their careers; so far his was unblemished, he would hate to see it go down the toilet.

Unfortunately, he had been in law enforcement long enough to have witnessed careers being ruined for less. So, he and Joe Bob agreed that in the beginning of the investigation, he would have to tread lightly and not step on his fellow law enforcement leaders' toes. After all, as they both were aware, Mena was a small town, and just about everybody was kin to someone there; he had to be damned certain the patrolman driving the vehicle was directly connected to the kidnapped girls. The last thing Brady wanted was to get into a pissing contest with the Mena Chief of Police.

Anyway, Ruby Lynn had already expressed concern about the jurisdictional issues. More than likely, as the mayor she would have to make the judgment call. If law enforcement believed the information Louie Youngblood had given them that the gathering would take place the next night, then time was of importance. They either had to stop the leak, or use the snitch to their advantage by relaying incorrect information to him, or her.

It did not take Ruby Lynn long to devise a solution how to handle the issue of the alleged bad cop. She instructed Brady to call the Chief of Police and tell him to make an announcement to all of his employees that, now that they had recovered the two missing girls from Waldron, there was no reason to come back to that area; their investigation had been concluded. Ruby Lynn announced to her team, "That should put anyone's mind at rest. Hopefully, they will let down their guard, and we can slip in unexpected."

Chapter 26
THE GATHERING OF THE "GOLDEN HAIRS"

Judah Green hiked back to his cabin. He was furious when he found out his "Golden Hair" was no longer there. The damn mayor from Waldron had snatched her right out from under his nose; but for the time being, Judah would have to put that incident on the back burner. Besides, he was on the cusp of his big night. He was in charge of the important gathering and he was reeling from excitement. The Elders had been the governing body for the three mountains for as long as anyone could remember.

Judah Green had talked to the men folk who had all agreed it was time for a change. All the mountain men had agreed to back him in his takeover of power even if he had to kill all three Elders. In order to do that, he had to have his wits about him. He wanted to impress the mountain men so he needed to look his best. So, he decided he was going to take a long overdue bath and shave for the special occasion. What the heck did he have to lose?

After he had groomed himself and put on his one set of clean clothes, he looked in the mirror and was quite pleased at his reflection. He was confident that everyone else would be impressed with his handsome appearance. He carefully took the three white ceremonial gowns from out of the crumbled brown paper sack; he smiled as he pictured his three daughters sitting by his side at the ceremony and how proud they would be of their daddy.

Judah was about to leave when someone knocked on his door. He fetched his shotgun and slowly cracked open the door. In all the chaos, it had slipped his mind that he had invited his Mena police snitch and former Waldron football team mate, Andy, to join in the celebration.

Judah was relieved when he saw that his not-so-bright friend had had the foresight to wear civilian clothes to blend in with the rest of the celebrants. Even though, he was a damn cop, he had served his purpose in Judah's master plan, therefore, he greeted him like a long-lost friend. Judah was excited as Andy eagerly shared that "The law ain't comin' up here no more." Pleased, Judah shook Andy's hand and promised him a good time tonight; he could pick any Golden Hair of his choosing that is except his own daughters who were to be untouched. Judah Green's vision was coming true. No one could stop him.

Chapter 27
TOP OF THE MOUNTAIN

At the top of Black Fork Mountain, Louie Youngblood had battled the snow and the freezing conditions to finally see Jenny and his daughter. His wife was in disbelief when she heard the sound of his voice resonating throughout the cabin. She ran to him crying and showering him in loving kisses. He was so relieved to see her that he took her in his arms, never wanting to ever let her go again, or face his knowledge it would only be a matter of time before the law came looking for him.

Louie explained what had happened when he had found Kitty with Joe Bob and Ruby Lynn at Judah Green's cabin, and he had reunited them with Maud. Next, he told her about how he had given them what information he knew about the gathering that was scheduled to happen. The biggest problem Louie could foresee, was not to arouse suspicion about his part in the disappearance of Kitty.

The other issue weighing heavily on his mind was that he, Jenny and Naomi would all have to be present at the gathering. It was clan custom; the Healer of the clan would make a special acknowledgement, presenting Jenny as their oldest Golden Hair.

Louie and Jenny agreed on a plan. Years ago, Jenny had found an empty cave hidden deep in the mountain near her cabin; and if they got separated they were to meet there. Louie was standing in back of her as she looked into the mirror, her blue eyes grew dark as she spoke, "Husband, I will not be taken, I would sooner die than leave my home."

His voice shook, "I know."

Louie was almost positive violence would break out once the rescue team found the meeting, and the mountain men. Louie only hoped the rescue team would get there in time. Jenny nervously dressed in her white gown. She stiffly sat while Louie brushed her hair and plaited it in a long braid trailing down to the floor. Each time they looked into each other's eyes their love for one another feverishly deepened. Tonight, they each had a part to play and they had to remain in control. No one must guess their secret: that Louie had told law enforcement about the gathering.

Chapter 28
THE CEREMONY

The ceremony was about to commence. Standing on a rock cliff high above everyone, one of the Elders proclaimed, "This is a great day! It is the first time since the Great Depression that all the "Golden Hairs" from the three mountains have been called together." The men cheered and fired their rifles in the air celebrating the union.

Louie Youngblood and Jenny were standing on the precipice and Jenny was holding their daughter close to her body. He scanned through the crowd and saw the poor women huddled together. It was becoming more difficult for him to remain desensitized. There were females of all ages, all with two important factors in common: each had the hair of Gold and the eyes of Blue.

Before the torches were lit, the Elders demanded, "All the Golden Hairs will be bathed and ready for trading. The Healer will accompany them to Big Creek." The group silently followed Louie down the trail to the stream. He tried not to wince as he watched the group disrobe and mutely step into the chilly creek bed. Each had brought her ceremonial white gown. Louie was told to check the females for sores, lacerations or infections; but to his dismay, there were too many injured to doctor. The Elders had given him only an hour to go to the creek, have the Golden Hairs bathed and changed into their gowns, and he had still not spotted the woman that resembled his Jenny. Due to time restrictions, he was forced to narrow down his healing to the most severe cases. Just as his ancestors, Louie had always been a strong man; but seeing the ghastly bruises on their beaten bodies made him ill. It was evident that most were half starved, the way the skin stretched tight to their rib cages, showing their bones. Louie Youngblood had seen many horrible things in his life, but this display of inhumanity was the worst he had ever encountered. He sadly turned away from the females to give them privacy, and to give himself time to control his anger.

After the Golden Hairs finished bathing, they dressed and formed a line to go back. It was as if they were already dead. From the lack of expression on each face, Louie deduced that, more than likely, each had been beaten into submission and had given up, not caring what their fate would be next.

Upon their arrival, men in the circle lit their torches, giving the ceremonial arena an almost mystic feel. The cool breeze teasingly swept through the air, entwining the yellow burst from the flames and shining golden flakes on the curls of the Golden Hairs long blond locks.

One of the three Elders commanded the Golden Hairs to sit. Passively, each sat down upon the ground. Each of the mountain men stood up acknowledging the Golden Hairs power then crowd immediately grew quiet, one of the Black Fork Elders, clad in a black robe, spoke. "Welcome, our Brothers from Rich Mountain Clan and Ouachita Mountains Clan." He motioned for Brother Green, who was standing beside him, to come forward. The Elder carried on, praising Judah Green. The Elder told how Judah had singlehandedly created this dynamic plan to gather everyone together for the meeting and exchange of "Golden Hairs".

Green stood fidgeting, anxious to speak. He waved to the crowd, and the men roared in anticipation. He raised his hands theatrically up into the air and shouted, "We are all brothers and equals! It is a new day and a new time! The old ways are a thing of the past!" His eyes grew dark as he drew the knife blade from his boot and pointed to the Elders. "We do not need old men tellin' us what to do!"

The crowd grew silent as all eyes focused on the make shift stage. In disbelief, the three Elders stood frozen. Before they had time to react,

Green viciously slit each of the Elders' throats. Jenny gasped as the blood spread over the rock surface and spilled onto her bare feet. Bewildered, and having witnessed this horrendous act, Louie grabbed Jenny, shielding her and Naomi's eyes in the hope that Green was through with this madness.

Judah Green's eyes narrowed and his lips twitched, as if an evil force had suddenly taken over his body. He licked the blood from the knife and forcefully threw it into the crowd of men. Judah laughed as he observed the men diving to the ground and attacking one another. The blood flowed from their struggle as each fought to retrieve the prized possession. The winner jumped up, holding the knife. Ceremoniously, Judah bade him to join him on the rock platform.

Relishing his new role and his new power, Judah roared, "Rise! Golden Hairs! It is time for the bidding." He looked down into the crowd and summoned his three daughters to the platform.

Bewildered, his oldest daughter looked up at the platform, searching for guidance. Jenny saw the fear in her eyes intensifying Jenny's horrible feeling. She was afraid they had been cast into a vile nightmare. Stiffly, Jenny gestured for Judah Green's three daughters to come and stand beside their father. He leaped down the rocks, guiding his daughters up to the platform for all to see their beauty. He was ecstatic. His diabolical plan was going even better than he had expected.

Meanwhile, the extraction team had come in soundlessly through the wicked landscape. They had heard the echoes carried through the night and had eventually been able to locate the source of the smoke that filled the air. The extraction team was under explicit orders to remain in blackout mode; all the team's communication devices had been switched off and were to remain silenced. Before leaving base camp, all of the lawmen's faces and helmets had been applied with camouflage face paint in a disruptive pattern. It was essential to the success of the operation; each would need to blend into the environment.

The team's mission was to get in and out as quickly as possible, and to avoid harming the kidnap victims in the process, their task was to get them immediately to safety. The snipers, their best trained marksmen, were the first tier to go in. They were under orders to set up position on the bluffs and cover the movements of the extraction team. The second tier would be responsible for the extraction of the girls, and the last team would be manned with firepower.

Joe Bob and Brady were assigned to the snipers, and Slade was on the third team. The plan sounded good in theory, but everyone in the command center at base camp was waiting with bated breath for positive results. All personnel involved had set their watches, and each had a designated time.

The snipers penetrated the woods. Joe Bob swiftly climbed to the top of the cliff, flattening his body and crawling to the rocky edge. He was so keyed up that it was difficult to slow his heart rate down. He placed his Remington 700 into the fold of his shoulder and took a deep breath. He adjusted his scope. Bingo, he had a straight line shot directly at the targets on the ground. He scanned the area, and immediately noted another level, situated higher above the rest. Through his scope, he saw the blood and the three dead bodies slumped on the rock surface. He hoped maybe the bastards were already turning on each other.

Joe Bob moved his scope a little farther left and saw Louie Youngblood; and a woman with a child, standing on the rock beside him. Joe Bob swung his scope down into the crowd and saw the females standing in a circle. He looked down at his watch. His nerves were on edge; extraction would begin in the next minute. He saw the first squad enter the perimeter. The women and children would need to be taken before they climbed upon the higher rocky surface, or they all could be used as human shields. Joe Bob sighted the rock platform, ready to shoot.

As supernatural as it seemed, Joe Bob could have sworn that the Indian sensed his presence. Youngblood looked directly at the sniper and slightly nodded his head toward the man standing to his right, who fit the description of Judah Green, only clean shaven. Without thinking, Joe Bob had zeroed in on Green, when he realized the three girls standing next to him were the ones he had seen previously at the cabin. The Golden Hairs were all now standing in a long line. Joe Bob watched as the second team moved in and, without anyone noticing, took a few of the girls located at the end of the line and leaving the rest. The big guns were waiting for the extraction team's signal if anything went south.

The extraction team was able to rescue five girls before they were detected; and then all hell broke loose. The fireworks started. Everyone started running in all directions, diving into the brush for protection. The mountain men aimed their weapons into the sea of lawmen.

All communications got the green light. Walkie-talkies were blaring with precisely organized instructions to take out specific targets. The extraction team bravely rushed in, dodging bullets to save the women and the children, physically picking each one up and leaving them sheltered in the safety of the trees.

Before Joe Bob squeezed the trigger, he saw Louie Youngblood protectively throw his body over the woman and the child next to him, knocking them off the rock and away from the gunfire. Joe Bob fired the shot. His bullet ripped through the target, and Judah Green teetered and started slowly falling, attempting to take his eldest daughter with him into the depths below.

Joe Bob watched helplessly as the girl frantically tried to tear her hand away from Judah Green's grasp. In one last effort, she stretched out her hand and reached for Louie Youngblood; he caught her hand and pulled her up onto the rock. Using his body to shield her and the other two girls from the impact of the fire power, he remained in front of them. The incoming shots battered his body. Louie Youngblood did not waver; he bravely stood until his body could endure no more. He collapsed onto the rock.

At the exact moment, he closed his eyes for the last time, Louie Youngblood heard the sound of the lone wolf howling, echoing through the tall pines, mourning the loss of his master. As was their plan, Jenny and her child were heading to the cave for protection, but Judah Green's girls jumped down off the rock screaming. Jenny quickly grabbed the three girls leading them to safety. In his rifle scope, Joe Bob watched them break away from the mayhem, and escape into the woods.

At the base, on the edge of the forest, Ruby Lynn had been impatiently waiting for news. Alarmed, she heard the unmistakable sound of gunfire rumbling over the mountain. Her muscles ached with tension as she closely monitored the chatter on the radio, waiting to hear Joe Bob's voice. She felt confident that he was safe, but she would have to see for herself.

Ruby Lynn grabbed her flashlight; then she drew her weapon and charged ahead, clearing a path. Unafraid, she ran through the underbrush, with a quick stride toward the sound of the chaos. Through a listening device in her ear attached to her portable radio, she heard, "Casualty count is high."

Talking to herself out loud, she clamored, "Oh, God. What if something has happened to Joe Bob?"

The buzz on the radio relayed the snipers were on their way back to base. But Ruby Lynn, needed to know the details about the extraction team.

She heard the radio chatter; something odd had happened to some of the women.

Brady screamed into the radio," Some of them are gone. One minute they were there and the next, they were gone! They were on the ledge and then, vanished into the night!"

She yelled into the radio, "How many do you have?"

Brady answered, "All but four and a baby."

Ruby Lynn could not believe her ears. How could the team have lost some of the kidnap victims? She ran deeper into the woods. She was struggling maneuvering her feet around the sharp rocks.

She had just stepped down when her ankle gave. Ruby Lynn lost her balance and fell roughly down an embankment, hitting her head and plunging her into the darkness. *Her vision was so vivid as the brilliant light spilled into the darkness. Mesmerized, Ruby Lynn watched as the beams of light caught mockingly on the shadows and bounced off the swaying tree branches with vivid streaks of yellow and blue, strangely setting fire to the dense woods surrounding her. She raised her hand and touched the spider-like patterns oddly covering the moon. She watched the four white shadows, with their ghost-like appearance, blending magically into the night as they wove sensuously in and out of the trees. The fading breeze caught their golden locks as they swirled their bodies impishly in the masked darkness.*

As the figures grew nearer, she could see their hollow faces with sparkling blue eyes jutting abnormally from their sockets. She watched as the apparitions silently started to pass by her. Impulsively, she reached out her arms; and she felt their warm bodies engulfing hers; their breath warm, screaming in her ears, lost forever. Dazed, Ruby Lynn was not sure if this mirage was one of her "Visions" or reality? of how she had gotten to this place. She awoke, to the faint sound of dripping water. The sparks from the fire cast a gloomy shadow on the glistening cavern walls, and were cool to the touch. Ruby Lynn watched the reflection of the four figures as they drew warmth from the glowing fire; their long flowing blond hair sparkling in the flames. Turning in Ruby Lynn's direction the face with piercing Sapphire eyes stared at her; called to her. Docilely, Ruby Lynn stood up and, touched the beautiful white gown she was wearing; surprised she looked down and her ankle was wrapped in a thin gauze bandage. She had no recollection of this unfamiliar place. Ruby Lynn moved closer to the face with the Sapphire eyes, and she pressed something into Ruby Lynn's hand. Ruby Lynn's eyes were still unaccustomed to the flame illuminating the darkness when she thought she saw Louie Youngblood standing in front of her; she reached out to him, but instead she felt the touch of warm fur on her fingertips. The giant wolf was magnificent, his brown eyes watched her closely as he moved toward her; gently nudging her from out of the cave, and into the bright sunlight. She did not fear the beautiful creature, and followed him as he glided magically among the trees, and guided Ruby Lynn to the edge of the forest.

Ruby Lynn started to open the folded piece of paper in her hand when she saw Joe Bob racing toward her; confused, she started to turn to get one last look at the beautiful creature, but the wolf was no longer there; he had vanished.

Shocked, Joe Bob saw his wife, oddly smiling and standing alone. Joe Bob was stunned at her appearance; her dark hair was loose and flowing gently down her back, and she was wearing a beautiful white gown.

Joe Bob pulled her into his arms and cried, "Ruby Lynn! Thank God! You are safe! Where in God's name have you been?"

Instead of answering, Ruby Lynn stared at her husband. She did not reply but handed him the piece of yellowed paper pressed in her hand.

Next, she smiled, and gingerly and took her husband's hand and like a child, she sat down in front of him smoothing out her white gown, and eagerly waiting for him to read the letter out loud. His voice quivered as he read, "Once upon a time, years ago in the mountains of Arkansas, life was riddled with hardship. Candles, coal oil lamps, and wood stoves were used in old run-down, one-room shacks hidden way deep in the pines. That was back when Arkansas winters were a might tough on the "Mountain People." Water was drawn and fetched from the wells by thin old women. Deer, squirrel and rabbit were hunted by the men folk. If you listened real close, you could hear the gaunt blue-tick hounds howling deep in the woods. Far in these back woods, people lived alone from the outside world. Rumor was that, when one of the women folk died, another female child would have to take her place; them was the rules! So, one of the men would have to slip right quiet like into town and snatch him a new bride. But all these brides had one thing in common because of the luck they would bring their new home. Every one of these child brides had to have hair the color of Gold and eyes of Blue, and nothing else would do."

The End

ACKNOWLEDGEMENTS

I'd like to thank Rachel Holladay-Coffman, Gail Marie Wilson-Wieland, Dr. Rhonda Fowler and Chris Dumas for your help and support.

I am grateful to my family and friends for all of your encouragement.

Thank you to the cities of Mena, Waldron, and Fort Smith, Arkansas for helping to ignite my imagination.

To all the men and women in "Blue" for your selfless acts of heroism.

Made in the USA
Lexington, KY
06 January 2017